There was no such thing as a simple kiss with ...iley...

There wa... ...raw force of a... ...much as it arou... ...s and who he w... ...the wall, hand... ...hair, he still couldn't get close enough.

In the late-night stillness of the hotel, he drew back for breath. "I want you tonight, Kat. And my room's right here."

"Handy," she murmured breathlessly, reeling beneath his passionate onslaught.

With one finger he raised her chin to look into her eyes. "So, what do you say?"

For once, she didn't know what to say. It was not propriety that stopped her. She wanted J. P. Harrington. Wanted him as much as he wanted her. She was too honest to deny that, and too honest not to set the record straight. "I...ah...don't want to get involved."

A smile played on his mouth. "You wouldn't be trying to save me now, Kiley, would you? Because I'm a big boy and I can take care of myself."

"Well, then," she replied, tossing her hair. "Why don't you open the door?"

J.P. turned the key, then quietly, wordlessly led her into the darkened room.

After a ten-year career in advertising, **Susan Worth** turned to her first loves—her family and her writing. She is presently hard at work on her third novel, and living in Virginia.

Books by Susan Worth

HARLEQUIN TEMPTATION
580—COMMITMENTS

Don't miss any of our special offers. Write to us at the following address for information on our newest releases.

Harlequin Reader Service
U.S.: 3010 Walden Ave., P.O. Box 1325, Buffalo, NY 14269
Canadian: P.O. Box 609, Fort Erie, Ont. L2A 5X3

HEART AND SOUL
Susan Worth

Harlequin Books

TORONTO • NEW YORK • LONDON
AMSTERDAM • PARIS • SYDNEY • HAMBURG
STOCKHOLM • ATHENS • TOKYO • MILAN
MADRID • WARSAW • BUDAPEST • AUCKLAND

To my editor Susan Sheppard,
for believing in this story.

ISBN 0-373-25760-0

HEART AND SOUL

1

THE FIRST TIME he ever saw her, J. P. Harrington felt the stirrings of admiration and the icy prickle of his own fear.

Her camera raised, the lone woman photographer crouched in the middle of an open field. Even as the jungle around them shook with the roar of incoming armored tanks, the woman clicked away with single-minded intensity. So intent, she seemed totally oblivious to the dangers of her exposed position.

The danger was something J.P. had to note.

At nearly forty, a third-generation foreign correspondent, J. P. Harrington had thought he'd seen it all, done it all. But he had to admit, he'd never seen a sight exactly like her.

"Who the hell is that?" he muttered to the man hunkered down beside him.

"Name's Kat Kiley." Paul Collins had covered as many battles as J.P. himself, but watching her, even the unflappable Australian's voice took on a note of awe. "She's new. A stringer for UPI. Good, isn't she?"

"She's crazy. Crazier than you are." And that was saying something. Still, J.P. couldn't seem to tear his eyes away, either.

"One of your countrymen, I believe."

Three cheers for Yankee ingenuity, J.P. thought. That is, if she didn't manage to get herself killed first. Technically, a foreign journalist was safe in a war zone—but try telling that to young, inexperienced troops who tended to shoot first, ask questions later.

Through the dense Central American foliage, the armored tanks rolled in. J.P.'s heart stopped beating. Trapped between the two front lines, the woman named Kat still snapped away. Within minutes, Kat Kiley would be totally cut off.

Beside him, Paul uttered a whispered prayer. Prayers alone, however, were not going to save her.

There was a code of honor among the international press, one J.P. held dear. Never leave your own, so the saying went—even if your own were completely out of their minds.

J.P. tossed down his gear. "Include me in one of those prayers, will you?"

The Aussie's eyes widened. "Blimey, you're not going after her?"

"Do you have a better plan?"

"No, but...here I thought I was the crazy one."

Paul sounded impressed enough to make J.P. glance his way. "You know, Collins, I think that's the nicest thing you've ever said to me. Put that in my eulogy, would you? Or better yet, make yourself useful and round up that press truck."

"Will do." Paul Collins glanced again at the scant distance between the woman and those armored tanks. "I just hope she's worth it, mate."

On that benediction, J.P. made his move. Sprinting across the open field, he closed the distance between himself and the woman. On a flying tackle, he sprang at her, catching her off guard.

Amid a swirl of dust, they toppled. J.P. caught a confused glimpse of wild red hair and even wilder green eyes. And she was young, so young J.P. caught his breath in shocked surprise.

It was a far greater shock when Kat Kiley started fighting back. Suddenly it was like trying to help a wild animal, a wild animal that didn't know it needed saving.

Mindless with fear, Kat instinctively fought for her life. If there were any benefits in surviving a tough childhood, fighting back was among them. Reflexively, mercilessly, Kat attacked. Like a street fighter, she pummeled with every weapon at her disposal. Knees, elbows, teeth.

For J. P. Harrington, a product of prep schools and Connecticut drawing rooms, it took every ounce of his considerable willpower just to hold her down.

But a one-hundred-and-twenty-pound woman, no matter how tough, was no match for a man nearly double her weight, particularly when that man refused to give up.

Grunting with the strain, J.P. swung one leg over her bucking torso, then pinioned her wrists above her head. He clamped his free hand over her mouth.

Trapped helpless beneath him, Kat thought of her mother then. Of her mother, scrimping and saving to buy her that first camera when she was fifteen. Of her mother, as trapped by poverty as by religious vows in a marriage that almost killed her. And last, of her mother's refusal to fight back.

Kat went very still.

Thinking her calm, J.P. shifted his hand. Only slightly, but enough for Kat to rear up and bite him, hard enough to draw blood.

"Goddamn it." J.P. stared in stunned disbelief at the teeth marks indelibly etched in his skin. Her teeth marks.

Beneath him, Kat stopped fighting in earnest. "You're American?"

"The *New York Times* seems to think so." J.P.'s gaze locked with Kat's wild green eyes. "J. P. Harrington. New York bureau. And I'd say it was a pleasure to meet you, but I happen to be trying to save you, you little idiot."

"Save me from what?" she hissed.

"From that." His hand still smarting, J.P. ruthlessly twisted her head to make her look behind him. The tanks were very close now, close enough to make him pale beneath his tan. Let her fight him again. This time he'd leave her. Then again, given the way Kat Kiley fought, she and a battalion were about evenly matched.

But J.P. had to hand it to her, once Kat Kiley finally got the picture, she recovered fast, faster than he did, for that matter. With the agility of her namesake, she rolled from beneath him and sprang to her feet.

"Mind if we save the formal introductions for later?" she tossed over her shoulder, already on the move. "I think it's time to make a run for it."

"What a fabulous idea," J.P. snapped, right on her heels. "Now why didn't *I* think of that?"

Crashing through the underbrush, they found the press truck waiting. Paul, God bless him. J.P. didn't think he'd ever been so grateful to see anything in his entire life as that crazy Australian, grinning broadly from the high cab. Like the true adrenaline junkie he was, Paul waved merrily. "Congratulations, mates. A grand adventure, eh?"

Just then there was a roar from behind. J.P. turned just in time to witness thousands of tons of steel marching over the field where seconds ago he and Kat had stood. Even as he watched, the tanks mindlessly obliterated everything and anything in their mechanical wake.

A grand adventure? he thought weakly.

"Get in, Harrington." Kat's voice came at him, urgent now. "This is no time to choke."

"Cho—" J.P. blinked. "Excuse me, wasn't I the one who saved you?"

But Kat had already gripped him by the sleeves and was unceremoniously hauling him over the rail into the relative safety of the truck bed.

"All set back there, kids?"

Paul was really enjoying this. As for himself, J.P.

could barely find his voice. "Light this candle, Collins. And don't brake until you hit New York."

The driver, a local boy who'd undoubtedly witnessed more fighting in his short life than the entire Western press corps combined, seemed to second J.P.'s motion. With a screech of protest from the aging clutch, the truck bounced off down the rutted excuse for a road.

Collapsing against the rocking truck bed, J.P. sent up a silent prayer of thanks to every god ever heard of. After nearly seventeen years of combat work, he'd had close calls before—but it was not something a person ever got used to. His heart still racing, he closed his eyes.

The whir of the camera made him open them again. He stared at the sight of Kat Kiley, barely winded, clicking away at the last vestiges of war.

Crazy. The woman was definitely crazy.

As if sensing his dark thoughts, her finger paused on the shutter. "Thanks for the rescue."

When he merely grunted, she spared him a glance. "You okay?"

"Yes." J.P. ran a shaky hand over his face. "Are you?" If memory served, he'd tackled her pretty hard.

The click of her camera answered him. Obviously, Kat Kiley was fine.

Well, that made one of them. J.P. realized only then he was angry—very angry, which made him angrier still because he was never angry. An even temper and a cool head were a foreign correspondent's stocks-intrade, traits he'd always prided himself on. At least until today.

Though he should have been working himself, J.P. studied her instead.

His first impression had been accurate. Kat Kiley was young. In her mid-twenties, he guessed, no more. And attractive, very attractive. Sexy, really, if that adjective could ever be applied to a woman wearing combat boots and jungle fatigues. And yet somehow she was. Tall and slim, it was her hair that captured most of his attention. The riotous mass of auburn curls gleamed like fire in the midday sun. That hair looked both untamed and unruly, or maybe that was the woman herself.

While she might not exactly look like your average, run-of-the-mill combat photographer, she certainly acted like one. Eyes focused, teeth clenched, she didn't seem to remember him at all. Or their close call.

J.P. shook his head. What was a sexy American redhead doing in the middle of a Central American jungle? And more to the point, how dare she so blithely risk both their lives?

"Got it." With a smile of satisfaction, Kat turned.

It was not a smile J. P. Harrington returned. But then if a full battalion didn't faze her, neither, it appeared, did he.

With the care that some women lavished on babies, Kat swaddled the camera in its case. "It's hot," she murmured, reaching for the bandanna around her neck.

"That's probably why they call it a jungle."

She glanced up at that. "Are you sure you're okay?"

"Fine." But J.P. watched as she used the bandanna to swipe at her glistening neck. He shouldn't have found the gesture sexy, he should have looked away, and yet somehow he couldn't seem to control either impulse. Instinctively, his gut tightened.

Kat Kiley caught him midstare. "Are you—"

"Do not ask me again if I'm all right," he snapped, embarrassment now warring with anger.

"All right, I won't."

"Good. Because, you know, you took a big chance back there."

"I suppose." She folded her arms around her knees. "I got some great shots though."

In that moment, J.P. wanted to save the troops the trouble and kill her himself. Only generations of good breeding stopped him from leaping across that truck and wringing her self-satisfied, if sexy, neck.

If it was hot in the jungle, it began to dawn on Kat that it was even hotter inside this truck.

Across her bent knees, she studied the man opposite her. Gray eyes, sandy blond hair and, despite the stubbles and stains of war, attractive. Very attractive in that coolly self-confident way that some people seemed inherently born with. Usually people with money. Not having had it herself, she recognized that at once. Kat also recognized something else. "You're mad."

"Oh, you're quick."

"Very mad."

"And you're very quick." His voice practically

dripped sarcasm. Like most people who were rarely urged to anger, when it came he didn't know what to do with it. "Tell me, what finally gave me away?"

"Your nostrils are flaring and you're practically breathing fire."

"Oh, really?" The description, though apt, hardly flattered him. "Well, you practically got us both killed."

J.P. all but shouted this last line, his cool-eyed and levelheaded attitude now long gone.

Kat could have pointed out that she hadn't exactly asked him to save her. But like most people who were accustomed to fighting, she believed in picking her moments. At this particular one, discretion seemed the better part of valor. "You're right," she conceded at length. "I owe you one."

"No, correction, you owe me a *big* one."

Right again. Considering, she narrowed her eyes. "Tell you what. How about if I let you have some of these photographs?"

Even through his anger, J.P. couldn't miss the pride in her voice. It was unmistakable. "How do I know they're any good?"

At the challenge, her jaw jutted. "They're good, Harrington. Believe me."

And somehow he did. "Even if they are," he said with a shrug, "I don't think your soul can be reclaimed for a couple of photographs. Even good photographs."

"My soul?" Those incredible green eyes widened. "How did my soul get into all of this?"

With deliberate casualness, he met her gaze. "That's

what they say in this country. When you save someone's life their soul belongs to you."

"Really?" Tossing her hair, she laughed. "Well, I
guess I need to be more careful."

"My sentiments exactly," he retorted swiftly. "Too
bad for both of us it's too late."

Head cocked, she studied him a minute longer. "You
know, you're pretty quick yourself." With an easy grin,
she held out her hand. "By the way, I'm Kat Kiley."

Now J.P. hesitated. By nature he preferred peace to
confrontation, but he liked the conditions of the truce to
be clearly defined. And he had the distinct impression
that Kat Kiley did not get his point. Yet.

Her hand still outstretched, her green eyes danced. "I
like to be on a first-name basis with all gentlemen who
own my soul."

That did it. "J. P. Harrington," he said easily, taking
her hand within his. "And the next time you decide to
kill yourself, would you mind leaving me out of it?"

She got the message loud and clear, her smile fading
quickly. "I didn't exactly ask you to save me, Harrington."

"No?"

"No. I can take care of myself."

"Oh, we certainly saw every evidence of that."

When she would have snatched her hand away, he
held on, amused despite himself. With her wild red hair
and even wilder green eyes, she looked like a hellcat, a
very sexy hellcat. And for the briefest moment, J.P. al-

lowed himself to wonder what all that heat and energy would be like channeled elsewhere.

Furious, Kat struggled against him. "Let go of my hand."

"In a minute." He was back in control and, he had to say it, enjoying himself immensely. "So tell me, Kiley, what were you planning on doing today if I hadn't come along?"

Bravado died a hard death. "Something would have turned up."

"Like what?"

He had her and they both knew it. In victory, he could afford to be generous. "That was a crazy stunt you pulled today, Kiley," he said more gently, "and, what's more, you know it."

But he had to give her credit, when backed in a corner Kat Kiley came out swinging. "Well, if I'm so crazy, Harrington, then how come you saved me?" Defiantly, she met his eyes.

She was so close he could count her freckles, so close he could feel her warm breath fan against his face. "Because you're too pretty to end up as cannon fodder. Besides, a human soul is a terrible thing to waste."

"Yeah, well..." She glared at him. "To tell you the truth, Harrington, I'm not sure I can afford your help."

She was quick, he thought again. Very quick. When he laughed, she snatched her hand away. Satisfied he'd made his point, J.P. let her go.

For long seconds they took one another's measure.

"It might have been a little dangerous," she finally conceded.

That had to be the most grudging apology he'd ever received. "Is it that hard to apologize, Kiley?"

"I'd rather face down a battalion."

"No, please."

When he held up a hand, her eyes shot to his. That quiet smile of J. P. Harrington's was lethal, Kat decided. Possibly more lethal than bullets. She infinitely preferred war—it was far safer. And yet somehow, almost despite herself, Kat found herself smiling back at him.

"So how about if we call a truce, Kat?"

"I'll concede to a temporary cease-fire."

Still smiling, he shook his head. "You don't give up, Red, but okay, I'll agree to those terms." Leaning against the truck rail, he closed his eyes. "What a day. First I almost get mowed down by a battalion only to get bitten by a redhead with an attitude."

"That'll teach you to play knight in shining armor, Harrington." Tossing her hair, her grin turned sly. "And I wouldn't have bitten you if you hadn't snuck up on me."

He opened one eye. "Careful, Kiley, we have a cease-fire, remember?" The adrenaline still coursed through his body, though from the close call or her company, even he wasn't entirely sure. J.P. did admit to curiosity. "So why are you a combat photographer, Kat Kiley?"

"Why not?"

"Kind of a dangerous line of work for a woman, isn't it?"

He'd already decided he liked the way her green eyes flared when she was aroused. He wasn't disappointed now. They practically breathed fire.

"Oh, and it's less dangerous for a man, I suppose. Excuse me, Harrington, but the last time I checked, bullets do not discriminate between the sexes. They may be the only things that don't."

Too late, Kat caught his smile. Her eyes narrowed. "You are quick, Harrington, but who's violating our agreement now?"

"So are you an adrenaline junkie, Kat?"

"Hardly," she scoffed.

"Then why?"

"Do you always ask so many questions?"

"Of course. I'm a reporter."

"I'm not a story."

"Somehow, I doubt that. Come on, satisfy my curiosity. Why?"

"You don't give up, either, Harrington, do you?" But it came out like grudging approval, and Kat found herself giving in. "Because I like to take pictures, and I like to move around and call my own shots." Her eyes met his. "I'm not big on following orders."

"Yes, I had noticed that."

At his dry tone, Kat had to smile. "Besides—" she shrugged "—the conditions aren't great and the co-workers can be a little bossy, but combat pays pretty well."

J.P. had thought nothing Kat Kiley could do or say would have surprised him. He would have been wrong.

"That's why you do it?" He stared at her. "You took a chance like that...risked your life like that...for money?"

At his shocked tone, she laughed. "Spoken like a man who's always had it, Harrington."

J.P. couldn't entirely decide whether to be insulted or amused, and though he had the distinct impression he was playing with fire, he couldn't seem to help asking the next question. "And just what makes you say that, Kat Kiley?"

It was as if she'd already sensed that people rarely got the better of J.P.

Slowly, almost leisurely, her gaze circled him then, taking in the expensive cut of his combat clothing, the gleam of his Rolex in the midday sun. And when she looked up again, she wore a smile, a very smug smile. "Lucky guess."

In the face of that grin, J.P. couldn't quite decide whether to kiss her or kill her, an odd and somewhat confusing admission for a forty-year-old man, one accustomed to being in control. Drawing in a deep breath, J.P., at least, decided to play it safe. "You have an interesting way of showing gratitude, Kiley."

"So I've been told."

When she continued to grin at him, he shook his head. "That wasn't exactly a compliment."

"I know."

And this time, they both smiled.

Just then the press truck shuddered to a halt outside the hotel. Before J.P. could react, Kat stood. With practiced ease, she shouldered her heavy camera bag. "Thanks again for the rescue, Harrington." With the briefest of smiles, she started to hop out.

"Wait a minute. Wait a sec." Without thinking, J.P. swiped at the sleeve of her flak jacket to hold her in place. He'd done it instinctively. Just as instinctively, the fire was back in Kat's eyes.

"I've already thanked you, Harrington. Twice now."

"No." J.P. shook his head. "No, that isn't it. I wanted to know if you wanted to have a drink with me, tonight at the hotel?"

He said it quickly, before he could change his mind. While he might be quick, Kat was faster.

Her expression changed so rapidly only a trained observer could have seen it. *From the light of battle, to what?* he wondered. Was it wariness he saw now? Or was it fear? And before J.P. had time to figure out why a woman who so blithely risked her life for money should look so scared at the thought of a simple drink, the look was gone.

She tossed her hair. "I would have thought you'd suffered enough for one day, Harrington."

So would he. "How about seven o'clock? I'll pick you up at your room."

"You are a man of confidence, J. P. Harrington. But how 'bout no?"

"No?" Now J.P. was surprised. He knew he was at-

tracted to her, had thought she was attracted to him.
And though he waited for some explanation, it appeared he waited in vain. "That's it, just *no*?"

"You're right." For an instant, Kat's green eyes
gleamed anew. "No thank you."

And with that, she disengaged her arm from his and
walked toward the hotel. In her wake, J.P. stared after
her.

"You're welcome," he snapped through gritted teeth.
That is, once he'd managed to close his gaping jaw.

Who the hell are you, Kat Kiley? he wondered once
more. And what was a sexy American redhead with an
attitude doing in the middle of a Central American war
zone?

ALONE, KAT LET HERSELF into her room. J. P. Harrington
had unnerved her, unnerved her more than the war,
though she hated to admit to weakness of any kind.

Only the tough survived. That was a lesson Kat had
learned early on. Maybe the day she'd discovered her
mother's paintings, lying dusty and abandoned in the
attic, unappreciated and unloved just like the artist herself. Or maybe it was the day she'd found out why her
mother married the man who called himself her father.
She tried to imagine what it must have been like to be a
poor Catholic teenager who found herself pregnant,
pregnant with Kat herself. Or maybe it was the day Kat
realized that her mother would never fight back. Never.
No matter how abusive or how demeaning her alco-

holic husband was. No, Francine Kiley would always turn the other cheek.

Well, not the daughter. Kat was going to be a famous photographer and she was going to fight back. And nobody, not even a man with a quiet smile and a watch worth more than her entire wardrobe, was going to stop her. And heaven help any man who tried.

2

IN EVERY WAR ZONE, in every country, there is a hotel that caters to foreign journalists. Through bribes, extortion and other generally illegal means, the proprietors manage to keep the faxes running and the telephone lines humming—the tools that fuel the press, make it their home-away-from-home. But a well-supplied bar is what journalists most appreciate, and it was to the bar that J.P. headed after sending in his story and cleaning up.

Cozily lit, the room was a veritable United Nations of accents. Within these snug walls, it was hard to imagine that a war raged right outside the doors.

Well, at least one kind of war.

Though J.P. told himself he wasn't looking, he spotted Kat Kiley right away. Just remembering their morning's encounter, he shook his head. A man would need a strong ego—he recalled the closeness of those tanks—a very strong ego around her.

Yet, he couldn't seem to look away, either. Seated alone at the bar, even in fresh jeans, combat boots and a white T-shirt jauntily topped with a red bandanna, somehow Kat looked sexy. Her thick hair gleamed like fire in the ambient light. That wild mane made his hand itch to touch it.

J.P. could not recall being so powerfully attracted to a woman before. And never, he concluded ruefully, with so little reason. If Kat noted his entrance as she sat nursing her drink it was one of the better kept secrets in the Western hemisphere.

"Harrington. Over here."

Paul, at least, seemed happy to see him. In fact, as J.P. wended his way to the far corner where Paul Collins held court, the Australian seemed downright delighted.

"Your girlfriend's here, mate. Over there, by the bar."

"So I noticed." Settling into a chair, J.P. deliberately kept his voice even. "But I think the 'girlfriend' bit would be news to her."

"You giving up?"

"There's nothing to give up on."

Ordering a fresh round, a reporter from a London paper leaned in. "I sense a story here."

"No—"

But even as J.P. tried to head him off, Paul Collins, his supposed best friend, appeared only too happy to oblige.

"Oh, you missed it, mate. Why only this morning, John Wayne here—otherwise known as the strong but silent J. P. Harrington—rescued a fair damsel in distress, Kiley that is. Except instead of riding off into the proverbial sunset, they engaged in a small skirmish. Blood was drawn—our boy's—and by last body count, she won. And I do believe our cool-eyed, levelheaded

American friend here finds himself a little gun-shy and not liking it very much. You know how those Yanks prefer their battle lines—clearly drawn and easily won."

The Brit sighed heavily. "And to think I wasted the entire day on irrelevant matters like troop movements when I could have had a real scoop."

J.P. eyed the grinning faces around the table. "Thank you so much, gentlemen, and you in particular, Collins. You've now managed to destroy what little was left of my ego."

"What are mates for?" Paul grinned cheekily.

The conversation moved on then, turning to critical issues like the unrest in the Gulf and if the Yankees could really go all the way and take the pennant.

But try though he might to stop himself, J.P.'s attention kept veering toward that bar. Was it sheer sexual chemistry? he wondered. Or simply that Kat Kiley seemed so alone, alone even in a room crowded with people?

"I think I'll get a drink."

J.P. said it casually, so casually that, immediately, Paul's bright blue eyes gleamed.

"You're not giving up."

"Shut up," J.P. instructed his friend pleasantly. He took two steps toward her, then paused. "And by the way, if you see me go under, send in reinforcements."

"To war and to women." Grinning, Paul held up his glass in a mock toast. "And if there's a difference I've never seen it."

To a chorus of "Hear, Hear" and the sound of betting pools being formed, J. P. Harrington made his move.

THE BEST DEFENSE is a good offense. So saying, J.P. was armed and ready.

"This isn't a pass, a come-on or an invitation, Kiley. This is merely a thirsty man approaching a bar, a bar you happen to be sitting at."

"Harrington."

He chose to ignore the sigh in her voice, the very obvious sigh. "Well, at least you remember me. Mind if I join you?"

She hesitated long enough to make him squirm. Given his attentive audience, however, J.P. didn't intend to surrender, at least not without a fight. "Fine. I'll make the questions easier. I'm sitting." To prove it, he did just that, a move that made Kat Kiley's brows rise.

She drew in a deep breath. "It's a free country, Harrington."

"No, actually, it isn't."

When she smiled at that, J.P. forged on. "So, tell me, Kiley, are we supposed to be mad at each other, or something?"

"Why would I be mad at you?"

"I don't know. I'm still trying to figure you out."

"I told you before I'm not a story."

"I'll be the judge of that. And by the way, Kiley, you're buying me a drink. It's the least you can do for scaring ten years off my life."

Under Kat's amused gaze, J.P. signaled for the bartender. He'd earned this drink, he told himself. He knew he needed it. Kat Kiley was headier than an adrenaline rush, and somehow infinitely more terrifying than those tanks.

"I'll have whatever she's having."

Behind the bar, the dark-skinned young man hesitated. "Señor—"

The bartender glanced toward Kat. So did J.P. "What's the problem now, Kiley? Don't you think I can handle it?"

Whatever she was about to say, it was lost as she tossed her hair. "You're right, Harrington. You've earned this. Set him up, Miguel."

The clear, watery beverage looked innocuous enough. That is, until J.P. caught the gleam in Kat's eyes. He remembered that gleam well—memory made him wary. "What is it, exactly?"

"Live dangerously, I always say."

He just bet she did. He wondered if she knew the way her breasts strained against her T-shirt. He wondered if she was wearing a bra. Most of all, he wondered why he was wondering these things about a woman whose every word was a challenge to his male pride.

As if to prove it, Kat exchanged a wink with the bartender. "Where's your spirit of adventure, Harrington?"

That did it, he gulped it down. And instantly made a face. "It's plain tonic water."

Beside him, Kat grinned. "I just can't fool you, Harrington, can I?"

"Why..." J.P. swallowed the bitter, fizzy stuff. "Why are you drinking tonic water?"

"Because I don't drink."

That statement was unusual enough to make J.P. sit up. Between the alternating excitement and the boredom, most foreign correspondents imbibed to the point of excess. "Mind telling me why?"

This time he caught the gleam. This time J. P. Harrington was a little smarter. "No, I get it." He held up a hand. "You mind."

Eyes dancing, she inclined her head. "You are so quick."

J.P. drew in oxygen, something there never seemed to be enough of around her. "All right, I give up. Who are you, Kat Kiley? Who are you and what are you doing in the middle of a Central American war zone?"

Enjoying the confusion on his face, Kat laughed. "Why do you ask?"

"Oh, I don't know. I guess I don't meet many women who almost get a man killed, for money no less, then refuse to apologize and then proceed to trample said man's ego. And I've only known you for—" J.P. consulted his fancy watch, then whistled "—a mere five hours. Tell me, Kiley, what is it you do for your finale?"

"You probably don't want to know. And tell me something, Harrington, if I'm so terrible—which you'll notice I'm not denying—then why do you keep coming back for more?"

He leaned in close. "Why do you always answer a question with a question?"

Eyes sparkling, Kat leaned in closer still. "Do I? Really? This is fascinating. Tell me more."

"Okay." J.P. put his drink down on the bar. "I could ask something really stupid now, like 'Do you plan to give me a hard time all night?' But thanks, anyway, I've figured that one out all by myself."

Tossing back her hair, Kat laughed. "I'm sorry, Harrington. It's just that you make it too easy."

"And you have such a lovely way of apologizing. Although...I *did* get you to apologize, now didn't I?"

At the look of triumph in those gray eyes, Kat had to laugh. "Yeah, I guess you did."

"That's okay." J.P. laughed a little himself then. "I hate tonic water."

Turning to the bar, he ordered a drink, a real one this time. Even before Kat could congratulate herself on her near escape, he'd turned back. "So what is Kat short for, anyway?"

"Harrington." She groaned. "Give up."

"Come on, Kiley. I'm known for my first-rate interviewing skills, and you're blowing my reputation." *To hell,* J.P. thought, hearing the chuckles from the table behind. "Besides, after this morning you do owe me something."

Kat might have resisted that, what she couldn't seem to resist was that quiet smile of his. "If I tell you, will you tell me?"

"Sure."

"It's Kathleen."

"Kathleen, huh?" He sized her up, then shook his head. "Sorry, I'd stick to Kat."

"I plan to." Since it was actually Kathleen Moira, she turned the tables on him. "So what does J.P. stand for?"

"I'll never tell. Never. Nobody knows my real name."

"You fight dirty...Jason?"

He grinned. "Not even close, Kiley. And just getting a little of my own back." Which was about time.

"Jack? Joe?" With J.P. smiling at her like that, Kat found it hard to concentrate. Thoughtfully, she narrowed her eyes. "No, it must be one of those incredibly yuppie names. Let me see... How about Jefferson? You know, you look kind of like a Jefferson. Very upstanding, trustworthy, a true gentleman."

Kat Kiley had pretty well hit her mark. Of course, that did little to explain J.P.'s sudden less-than-gentlemanly urge to kiss her senseless, to kiss her until they were both senseless. In a public place, no less. But then, Kat wasn't like any other woman he'd ever met. Any other person for that matter.

As if to prove it, beside him she crowed, "That's it, isn't it? It's Jefferson! I knew it."

Surprising her, surprising himself, he leaned in then to capture a hank of her hair. "Keep it up, Kiley. You're flirting with danger."

She thought maybe they both were. He was so close, Kat swore she could see herself reflected in his eyes. So close she inhaled the clean, woodsy scent of his expensive cologne. So close she felt the overwhelming pull of attraction between them, the one she had not wanted to admit to ever since they'd first laid eyes on each other.

In that moment, in that instant, they might have been the only two people in that crowded bar. And J.P. seemed to feel it, too.

"Your hair's like fire, Kat Kiley," he breathed.

"Then don't get too close. You'll get burned." But her voice lacked conviction and she couldn't seem to move away.

"I'll take my chances." Smiling slightly, J.P. loosened his hold, winding a lock of fiery red around his finger. At his tender touch, something cold in Kat's heart started to melt.

Except Kat wasn't a woman to melt easily. Maybe he'd take a chance, but she wouldn't. The stakes were too high. Deliberately, she pulled away.

"I thought you believed in living dangerously," was his only comment. But he let her go.

"That's professionally, not personally." Still, the way her heart thudded unevenly in her chest annoyed Kat—and it frightened her. For all his gentlemanly ways, or maybe because of them, J. P. Harrington was a dangerous man. "And thanks for the reminder."

Throwing down several coins on the bar, enough to cover both their drinks, she shouldered her camera case and slid off the stool.

For perhaps the second time in his life, J. P. Harrington didn't have a clue as to what was going on. One moment she was there and the next, gone.

By the time he found his voice, she was already at the

door. "Where the hell are you going, Kiley?" he was forced to call after her.

"Outside. There's a war on, Harrington, in case you haven't noticed."

He certainly had, though not outside those doors. "You can't go out there, Kat. It's too dangerous."

He could almost see her backbone stiffen. "Then don't come."

With a toss of her hair, she slipped out through the swinging door, leaving J.P. to stare openmouthed after her.

"Crazy woman," he muttered. With a little bang, he set his glass down on the bar. No, Kat Kiley was more than crazy. She had to be the most difficult, prickly, impossible-to-understand woman he'd ever had the misfortune of running into in his entire...

"Your girlfriend's getting away again, mate. You're really going to have to start winning these battles."

Collins. Perfect. The light of battle in his own eyes, J.P. turned on his friend then. "She is not my girlfriend."

He enunciated every syllable, a distinction clearly lost on the imperturbable Australian. "Well, whoever she is, she's getting away. It's dangerous out there, J.P."

"Would *you* care to tell Ms. Kiley she can't do something? Please, be my guest." With exaggerated politeness, J.P. gestured toward the door. "I'd pay money to watch that."

"She's not my girlfriend."

J.P. drew in a long breath, a long steadying breath. Beneath Paul Collins's steady gaze, however, he felt himself start to squirm. That was the problem with being a gentleman—scruples. "Fine. I'll go after her." Even as he slid from the stool, J.P. returned Paul's smile with a dark scowl of his own. "Just don't be surprised if one of us comes back in a body bag."

"I'll keep my fingers crossed it isn't you."

J.P. moved toward the door. "Your confidence and your concern are duly noted."

"Hey." Clearly offended, Paul called after him. "I've got ten bucks riding on you, mate."

At J.P.'s look of disgust, Paul grinned. "That's a real sign of loyalty, Harrington. Everyone else bet on Kiley."

J.P. CAUGHT UP WITH KAT right outside the hotel. It was still light outside, and still steamy. Then again, that might have been the smoke rising off him. Camera poised, Kat was angling up a shot. He wouldn't have minded a shot himself, though he didn't have a photograph in mind.

"Kiley, come back inside. It's too dangerous out here."

Lowering the camera a fraction of an inch, Kat stared at the peaceful village. As children played, and native women chattered through their evening chores, the scene might have been taken from a *National Geographic* page. "You call this dangerous, Harrington?" she scoffed. "I'd say Times Square at noon is worse."

He admitted it was quiet. Too quiet. The absolute silence made the hairs on the back of his neck prickle. "Yes, but my instincts tell me something's going down. And when it does, you're not going to like it."

"Instinct? You mean, like women's intuition?"

Kat's voice held a laugh, one that made his jaw tighten. Amazing how fast she managed to do that. With effort, he hung on to control. "Kiley, I'm telling you, you can't stay out here."

"And I keep telling you, Harrington, I can take care of myself. Relax, Sir Galahad, you're off duty. Take the rest of the night off. In fact, feel free to take the rest of your life off."

When she would have walked away, J.P. grabbed her arm. He'd done it without thinking, but even as she stiffened, he maintained his hold. "You want to get yourself killed for a couple of photographs?"

Her green eyes flashed. Something about his logic, coupled with his proprietary hold, made her temper sizzle and flare. "Yeah, well, it's my life, isn't it, so stop butting in." She struggled against his grip, but he wouldn't let go. J. P. Harrington might be stronger than she was, but she intended to prove she was every bit as tough. Her gaze raked from his hand to his face. "Harrington, if you don't let go of my arm this minute I swear I'll bite you again."

With a muttered oath, J.P. threw up his hands. "Okay, you want to get yourself killed, crazy lady? Go ahead. See if I care."

Kat struggled against the red-hot pulse of temper as she strode away, kicking up dust. Only the sight of the children playing around the piazza captured her artist's eye and soothed her temper. Even dirty and bedraggled, the children giggled and laughed, these innocent

victims who had never known anything but war.
Through the camera's eye she wanted to portray the di-
chotomy of their lives, except she didn't dare get too
close. That was the photographer's greatest challenge:
to capture what was there without interrupting or
changing it.

Lost in her art, she didn't hear J. P. Harrington come
up behind her until he spoke.

"This isn't exactly war, Kiley."

"I know." But she had her private hopes and dreams.
Combat work might pay the rent, but photography as
an art owned her soul. Ever since she was a kid she'd
taken pictures. Behind the camera, she felt secure, and
in control; perhaps that was the only place she ever had.
Over time it had proved her salvation and preserved
her sanity. But it was also an expensive and heart-
wrenching master. So hard to get right, and so easy to
get wrong. Still, the faces of people fascinated her with
their secret hopes and dreams. Even when she wanted
to quit, she knew she never would—never could, really.
"I have my own projects on the side."

"Ever had a show?"

"No." She felt rather than saw his brow rise at her
terse reply. "I'm not that good, really. It's just a hobby."

"I doubt that. You strike me as the kind of woman
who'd be good at whatever you set out to do."

"Thanks." Kat was touched and pleased by the compliment—more than he'd ever know, considering this
virtual stranger had shown more confidence in her than
her family ever had. She could almost hear her father's

sneer. "You still wastin' time with that photography crap?" With difficulty, Kat pushed the voice aside, suddenly remembering that she was angry at J. P. Harrington. "What are you doing out here, anyway?"

He stubbed at the dust with a booted foot. "I'm not sure, exactly."

She kept her eye trained on the lens. "Not still trying to save me, are you?"

When he didn't seem to have an answer for that question, either, she returned to her subjects.

The unfamiliar whir of the camera eventually disturbed the children. Fascinated by the sight of the two Americans, they crowded in close, showing amazing trust for a people who had never known anything but violence. Giggling, they pulled on Kat's jeans. One brave little soul even reached for her camera.

"Oh, no. You can't touch."

The little guy didn't understand a word. Then again, neither did Kat as a spate of rapid-fire Spanish came back at her. "Wait a minute. Wait. Not so fast."

"He wants to return the favor and take your picture."

Resigned, Kat turned to J.P. "Rescuing me again, Harrington? And, of course, you're fluent."

"Of course."

"Any other languages I should know about?"

"Oh, French, Italian, German and enough Russian to get by. Impressed?"

"Very. Prep school?"

He grinned. "I'll never tell that, either."

On a sigh, Kat considered first the man, then the boy.

She admitted to being at a distinct loss as to how to handle either. "Do you have any idea how much a Hasselblad costs, Harrington?"

In his educated Spanish, J.P. explained the situation. For a moment, the little guy looked disappointed, and then he giggled.

Eyes narrowed, Kat surveyed the tall man beside her. "What exactly did you tell him?"

"Oh, just that you were a crazy lady. Funny thing, he seemed to buy that right away."

"Thanks a lot, Harrington. I knew I couldn't afford your help."

They grinned at one another then. Only the clamoring of the children interrupted. Laughing, Kat doled out a handful of coins among them, their reward for being such good subjects. By American standards it wasn't very much money, but here, Kat knew it could feed an entire family for a week. Awed, they stared down at their bounty. It was more money than most of them had ever seen in their lives.

J.P. smiled. "You look like the Pied Piper, Kiley."

"I feel like one." She stared down at the pleased faces of the children, then looked around the peaceful square. "It's hard to believe there's a war going on here."

"Believe it," was his only comment.

And J.P. was right. In this country, war was never very far away.

The children heard it first. At the faint rumbling of armored tanks, they scattered, like animals in the forest seeking shelter.

Suddenly alone in the middle of the square, Kat's own instincts made her turn to the man beside her. "What the hell's going on?"

"Looks like the party is over." But J.P.'s voice had tensed. Grabbing her hand, he started to run. This time Kat put up no protest at his high-handed ways.

"Can we make it to the hotel?" Her voice came out on a gasp.

"Only as target practice. Care to risk it?"

"No thanks."

Neither did he. Ducking behind the shelter of an adobe building, he pulled her after him. Side by side, they watched as the troops rolled in. Within seconds, the tiny, peaceful town was overrun by tanks and men in uniform shouting orders.

It all happened so fast, Kat shook her head. "Now what?"

"Now we pray."

"Pray?" Her eyes shot to his. "That's the plan? I've always been more of a woman of action myself."

"Yes, Kiley, I've noticed that. We've all noticed that. But this time let's try it my way, all right?"

She might have protested further, except suddenly J.P. ground his body against hers. Kat found herself flattened against the wall.

"This isn't a pass," he whispered close to her ear.

"Thank you for sharing that."

"You're welcome."

The army passed so close Kat could see the expressions on the men's faces. So close that, instinctively, Kat inched for her camera.

"This is not a great time to wiggle, either, Kiley." He looked down at her. "Not scared, are you?"

"No." She met his eyes. "Actually, I was thinking of trying for a shot."

"A sho— Are you crazy?"

"Why do you keep asking me that?"

The army curtailed any response. Abruptly, the troops came to a halt, stopping right in front of their alleyway.

Kat swallowed hard. She reminded herself she wasn't scared. No, terrified was more like it. Without thinking, she pressed closer to J.P.'s side, instinctively seeking the warm shelter of his body.

Not that it would do much good if they were spotted.

Hardly daring to breathe, they waited. Though religion had always been a sore point in her life, Kat found herself following J.P.'s advice and offering up a few prayers of her own.

She was never quite sure if it was the powers above or just plain fate that intervened, causing the army to pick up and move again. As inexplicably and as suddenly as the tanks and troops had appeared, they disappeared again.

As soon as it was safe, J.P. grabbed her hand and started to run and the two Americans fled back to safety. Still, it was a much chastened Kat Kiley who reentered that hotel. She knew she couldn't ignore J. P. Harrington's blatant I-told-you-so expression.

"Looks like you were right, Harrington," she managed lightly.

"Looks like it."

If there was anything Kat hated more than apologizing, it was apologizing to a smug man. Still, she knew she owed him. "Sorry."

She should have known he wouldn't let her off the hook that easy.

"Excuse me, Kiley I...ah...didn't quite catch that."

"I *said* 'I'm sorry.'"

Her aggressive stance made him laugh. The squared shoulders, the fight in those green eyes. "Maybe from now on, you'll listen to me."

She cocked a brow. "*Maybe* I will."

The implication was that maybe she wouldn't. "That makes twice now, Kiley. This is getting to be a habit."

Yeah, a bad one. Kat didn't quite care for the gleam in his eye; it made her defensive and it made her nervous. "I think I'll turn in for the night. For once, I agree with you—life is exciting enough."

But when she would have turned away, he snagged her hand, pulling her back. "Not so fast, Red. You owe me. Again."

Even as her heartbeat quickened, sheer, raw courage made her face him. "What do you want now, Harrington? Sorry, but my soul's already gone and I'm fresh out of money."

"An interesting dilemma. Tell you what, I'll settle for a dance."

"A dance?"

For once, J.P. had caught her by surprise, a fact he noted with no small amount of satisfaction. "Yeah, you like Motown?"

"Motown?" Laughing, she shook her head. "We're in the middle of Central America, Harrington, and I don't hear any music."

"Trust me...you will."

Trust, particularly trust in men, had never been Kat Kiley's long suit. With her hand tucked securely in J.P.'s, however, she didn't seem to have much choice in the matter. But then she wasn't sure she'd ever had much choice where this man was concerned. And that was the scariest thought of all.

IN THE MIDDLE of a Central American jungle, in the middle of a war zone, the sounds of the Drifters and the Spinners and the Temptations stirred the senses even as they beguiled the soul.

Out on the dance floor, Kat had to laugh. "This is crazy, Harrington."

"I know." It suited Kat to a T. J.P. decided he liked the way her body moved, and the way her eyes smiled up at him, and in a mellower moment, he even decided he liked the way she gave him a hard time. And when Paul Collins tried to cut in, he good-naturedly brushed him off.

"Get your own date, you pushy Australian."

As Paul drifted off with a knowing grin, Kat stopped moving. "This isn't exactly a date, Harrington."

Not that J. P. Harrington listened. Deliberately, he

went to the jukebox, and even more deliberately selected one particular song. As the strains of "Heart and Soul" filled the room, her eyes found his.

"Very cute, Harrington."

"You finally noticed."

Brooking no arguments, J.P. pulled her into his arms. "You know I don't think I've ever slow-danced with a woman in combat boots before."

"That's okay, I don't think I've ever danced with a preppie before." But even as she said it, she smiled.

"All right, Kiley, that's it. I'm getting even." In his own way, he did. Drawing her tightly against him, he molded the long length of her body against his own. He could get used to this, he decided, combat boots and all.

And Kat thought maybe she could, too. In his arms, she felt safe, secure and protected, sensations she'd never found before anywhere in this world. It was an odd thing to feel in the middle of a war zone. Even odder, when pressed against a body that made her blood rush and her knees sag. J. P. Harrington had the ability to arouse complicated reactions within her. Reactions even Kat herself didn't understand.

She wasn't sure when one song ended and the next began, but she couldn't seem to care very much. Bodies swaying, they danced to a beat that had nothing to do with the rhythm of the music.

"It's late," he finally murmured against her hair.

"I suppose it is." Looking around, Kat was surprised to find the room empty and the bartender eyeing them over a yawn.

"Have a good time?"

She smiled up at J.P. then. "Motown in Central America. You know, Harrington, you can be pretty crazy yourself."

"Why, Kiley—" he feigned shock "—that wouldn't actually be a compliment, would it?"

"Don't push your luck, J.P."

But he thought he might. He thought he just might. One arm locked about Kat's waist, he escorted her up the stairs. With each step, her camera clacked against his side.

Somehow, J.P. felt as if he'd known her all his life and yet, he reminded himself, he didn't really know her at all. That was something he intended to remedy. "So where are you from, Kat? That is, when you're not dancing up a storm in the middle of a jungle."

When she answered without hesitation, J.P. knew he'd made real strides.

"Uptown Manhattan now, but I grew up in Connecticut."

"Really?" Pleased, he tightened his grip around her waist. "I'm midtown, but I grew up in Connecticut myself. Small world, isn't it?"

Not that small. With a little smile, Kat surveyed the expensive cut of his clothing, then thought of the depressing factory town the Kileys called home, the town she couldn't have escaped too soon. "Not the same part, I'll bet."

Catching the amusement in her voice, he looked

down at her. "And just what makes you say that, Kathleen?"

"Oh..." She tossed her hair. "Lucky guess."

As they rolled to a stop outside her door, her green eyes gleamed wickedly.

"You think you have my number, don't you, Kat Kiley?"

Leaning against the wall, she eyed him knowingly. "You bet I do...Jones?...Jared?...Jebediah?"

Weight supported on his arms, J.P. leaned in, trapping her between his body and the wall. "You're all wet, Kiley."

"I don't think so...Jehosophat?"

There were several ways to silence a teasing woman. J.P. picked the one he'd wanted to try ever since he'd first laid eyes on her.

As his lips came down toward hers, Kat leaned in to meet him halfway.

There was no such thing as a simple kiss with a woman as complicated as Kat Kiley. What started out as teasing quickly metamorphosed into more, much more. There was hunger here and heat, and the raw force of attraction shocked him almost as much as it aroused him.

In his near forty years, he had never shared a kiss like this. And if it was control he sought, J.P. didn't find it now. Instead of answering questions, their kiss only raised more.

He forgot where he was and who he was. Ramming her body against the wall, hands fisted in her hair, it still wasn't enough. He couldn't get close enough. In the late-night stillness of the hotel, he drew back for breath. "I want to come in tonight, Kat."

He was so close his warm breath fanned her cheek. Pulling back slightly, breathless herself, Kat was gratified to note that J. P. Harrington looked every bit as dazed as she felt. Her insides were churning, and it was hard to think with his body pressed against hers. She forced her head to clear. "I...ah...don't let anyone see my work before publication."

Nibbling at her neck, he was more than willing to compromise. "There's always my room."

So there was.

His teeth skimmed down her jawline. "I'm right next door."

"Handy," she murmured.

But for once, she was unable to hide behind her quick wit. With one finger, J.P. raised her chin to look into her eyes. "So, what do you say, Kat?"

She didn't know what to say. It was not propriety that stopped her. She wanted J. P. Harrington. Wanted him as much as he wanted her. She was too honest with herself to deny that. But her basic sense of honesty also compelled her to go on, and set the record straight. "I...ah...don't want to get involved."

He smiled at that. "You wouldn't be trying to save me, now, Kiley, would you? Because, you know it's my life and I happen to be a big boy. I can take care of myself."

Despite herself, Kat had to laugh. And make up her

mind. "Well, then," she murmured, tossing her hair. "Why don't I come in?"

"Why don't you?" Then, taking her hand, J.P. quietly, wordlessly, led her into the darkened room.

3

WHAT MIGHT HAVE BEEN awkward, even uncomfortable, back in the States, seemed almost natural in this country where nobody knew what tomorrow would bring, or if it would come at all. Or maybe it was the woman herself that made it feel so right.

When J.P. kicked shut the door with a booted foot, Kat smiled slightly. "I always wanted to do that," he confessed, catching her look.

"Yeah?"

"Yeah."

"This must be your night for fantasies, Harrington."

He thought it just might. Only the light of the moon through the window illuminated the room. When he hesitated at the light switch, Kat reached out to still his hand.

"I've been wanting to do this, too." Closing the scant distance between them, J.P. slid his hands around Kat's waist and drew her near. Even through the dim obscurity of the room, unerringly he found her lips.

As Kat wound her arms about his neck, the bite of her camera case pierced his ribs, catching him right below his heart. "May I?" J.P. breathed, not allowing either of them to break contact.

"Allow me."

In a gesture as provocative as a striptease, Kat eased the strap from her shoulder. The case hit the floor with a thud, much like the thud of J. P. Harrington's heart.

"Better?" Kat murmured.

Than what? J.P. wondered, dazed. The invitation in those green eyes or that wicked little half smile that curved her lips?

Almost blindly, he reached for her again. They kissed, wildly, crazily, hungrily.

Kat's uninhibited response made his blood heat. If she was fire, then he was fire, too. He felt as if he were ablaze.

Heedless now, his lips burned a path down her velvety skin. Beneath his touch, her pulse jumped wildly, echoing his own.

Still not satisfied, J.P. sought the fullness of her breast. As he kneaded and caressed, the cotton T-shirt slipped sinuously through his fingers.

Against him, Kat moaned low in her throat, her hands raking his back, as though trying to get closer still.

He was, J.P. realized, fast slipping out of control. With every ounce of willpower he had, he dammed the flow of raw need and told himself sternly to slow down. He reminded himself that he was not a man to take a woman easily or lightly, and especially not this woman. He raised a gentle hand to her cheek. Her skin felt heated to the touch, making him long for more.

Stepping back a little, he forced his head to clear. "Do

you...ah..." Strangled, he tried again. "Do you...want to sit down or something?"

"No. Do you?"

He heard rather than saw Kat's amusement. He supposed he couldn't entirely blame her for that. His effort to play host had come too late. "Not exactly, but..." *But what, Harrington?* For a man who made his living from his skill with words, why was he finding these simple ones so hard?

"Well, I don't usually go around attacking women, Kat. I...ah...just thought maybe you'd want to know that."

Her expression softened. "I believe you. And if it makes you feel any better, I don't usually go around attacking women, either."

"How about men?" he heard himself ask.

When she stiffened against him, he could have kicked himself. He knew if she stopped touching him now, he would kill himself. And yet the issue was his business, too, if they planned to get intimate.

Something Kat seemed to understand. "No," she said simply. "I don't usually let people get this close."

It was, he thought, the perfect answer, made even more perfect when she wound her arms around his neck and sought his lips again.

And yet still, he girded himself against temptation. "Are you sure about this?"

Her warm laughter bubbled against his lips. "You really do have iron control, don't you, J. P. Harrington?"

His body aching, the wry humor of the situation finally got the better of him. "No, I wouldn't say that. It's just...I want you to be sure, that's all."

"Tell you what, Harrington." Through the moon-dappled dimness of the room, Kat's voice caressed him. "I can see I'm going to have to attack you. That way we'll both feel a lot better."

Kat Kiley was as good as her word.

Even as her lips claimed his, J.P. was lost and he knew it. Like a drowning man going down for the third time, he gripped her hair and finished what had started between them out in a war zone in the middle of a Central American jungle.

They never even made it to the bed.

The joining of their two bodies was like an explosion. Kat had no rational explanation for the force of attraction between them, but it had been there ever since they'd first laid eyes on each other. And she was too honest with herself to deny even something she couldn't understand and was powerless to control.

Fearless was what J.P. thought, was all he could think. Kat Kiley was as fearless in her lovemaking as she was in everything else—and every bit as good. With single-minded determination, she turned her attention on him. This time, since he was the object of her concentration, he couldn't seem to find one single complaint about her risk-taking.

Impatient with the barriers between them, her agile fingers tugged at his shirt even as his found the edges of her T.

This was too fast, he thought, too reckless, too impatient. He scarcely recognized himself in this man who grappled and tore. He wanted to slow down, wanted to savor and caress, but he couldn't seem to stop the mad rush, either. For once in his life, he was desperate, desperate to hold and to taste and to possess. Control slipped and ebbed as he gave himself over to pure feeling.

They breathed hard, as the layers separating them were skimmed away. Amid the rasp of zippers and tugging of boots, he stifled a laugh.

"This might be easier if we weren't dressed for combat." But he scarcely got the words out.

"Hurry," was her only reply.

Try as he might, he couldn't seem to do anything else, until finally, bare flesh touched bare flesh.

In the hot thickness of the Central American night, their discarded clothing pooled at her feet, Kat Kiley stood like some pagan goddess. Bathed only in the light of the moon, her tousled hair streamed down her back and her green eyes shone. At the sight of her, J. P. Harrington forgot to breathe.

"God, you're beautiful."

She *was* beautiful. More beautiful than any woman had a right to be. More beautiful than any woman he'd ever seen.

"*Sshh.*" Kat sank to the floor and, in one fluid motion, she brought J.P. down with her.

He had to admit he didn't fight too hard. Mindful of his weight, he tried to brace himself.

Kat laughed, a breathless sound. "You're a hard man to seduce, Harrington."

"Try me."

Seeming to take that as a challenge, she did. With eyes glowing, she locked her legs around him, holding him prisoner, a willing prisoner.

Heat swirled in the room, a heat that had nothing to do with the temperature of the jungle, but from friction—the taut friction of two bodies straining hungrily. Their hands explored, racing frantically from throat to hip. When J.P. followed the same course with his mouth, the bite of Kat's nails raked his back.

Pleasure and pain intermingled. He felt velvety skin and the toned body of a woman who lived dangerously, a woman who took J.P. to an exquisitely dangerous place he had only dreamt about before.

Kat arched against him, wordlessly, soundlessly; a sight J.P. found as beautifully graceful as it was arousing.

And looking down at her then, the moonlight full on that incredible face, J. P. Harrington knew only one thing—he had never felt for a woman what he felt for Kat Kiley right now. Never.

He could not have put that feeling into words; it was too different, too new to him.

As if sensing his thoughts, Kat's lids fluttered open. At his expression, a hint of fear entered her eyes.

J.P. could almost understand that; he felt it himself. He had a premonition of danger, a sense that somehow their lives were spiraling out of control.

He knew he should ask her then if she'd changed her mind. Somehow he couldn't bring himself to—almost afraid of what she would say.

Instead he lowered his mouth to hers again, and quickly, so quickly, passion overruled logic and heat blocked out fear.

J.P. would have prolonged this moment forever, the feel of her skin pressed damply against his own, the fiery touch of her hands against his body, the mind-altering, logic-defying fire that scorched them both, but Kat urged him on.

Even as he slid into her, he knew the perfectness of the fit. Around him, so hot, so tight he almost lost control at once. Kat's answering moan shuddered from her lips to his own.

It was as if they'd been together forever. In that instant, he felt as if they had.

And yet even lost in sensation as J.P. was, one clear thought penetrated.

In a country torn by war and far away from his own, J. P. Harrington felt as if he'd found home, here, within Kat Kiley. He wondered if she felt it, too, but, true to her character, Kat Kiley gave little away. Even at the height of her passion, eyes glazed, head thrown back, she called out only one thing and only one syllable. "Oh," was all she said. He supposed he'd have to be satisfied with that.

But then whatever she chose to give, in that moment, Kat Kiley was more than satisfying him.

THE ROOM WAS SWATHED in velvet darkness, silent except for their unsteady breathing. J.P. was afraid to move, afraid he'd somehow break the spell.

Beside him Kat shifted, an almost restless motion that made him turn his head. "You okay?"

Kat didn't know *what* she was—a terrifying realization for a woman as focused as she had always been, had always had to be. What they'd just shared left her stunned and dazed. She was not sure she liked feeling either.

"Kathleen?" Propped on one elbow, J.P. levered himself to look at her.

Above her, those gray eyes of J. P. Harrington's were tender now. That scared Kat even more. She forced herself to smile. Even more deliberately, she lightened the mood. "Well, you asked what I did for my finale, Harrington."

But J. P. Harrington would never give her an easy out.

"That didn't feel like a finale to me," he murmured. "More like a beginning." When Kat would have looked away, he held her face near. "Did I hurt you?"

"No," she said softly. Not in the way he meant, anyway.

Gently, J.P. reached out to trace the line of her beard-chafed cheek, to caress the faint puffiness of her lips. "I think you do make me crazy. Sorry."

More moved by his touch than she cared to be, more frightened than she wanted to admit, Kat caught his hand, stilling it. He only linked his fingers around hers.

"I have to go."

"Why?" J.P. tightened his grip.

Because he was getting too close. Because he was scaring her. Because she never spent the night. It was one of her rules, like never letting anyone see her private work. "Because it's late," was what she settled on. "And besides, this floor is getting kind of hard."

Unable to argue with her there, J.P. rose, then held out a hand to help her up.

"Thanks."

But when she would have broken the contact, he hung on. "Hey, you're not involved with anyone, are you?"

J.P. found it both irritating and awkward that he had to ask, especially when Kat laughed. "It's a little late to be asking that, Harrington, isn't it?"

"Maybe." In retaliation for that laugh, J.P. caught a lock of fiery red and tugged her face near. That hair was too much of a temptation to resist. "I'd still like an answer, Kathleen."

There was a wicked little gleam in her eyes. "What does J.P. stand for?"

With a strangled sound, he pressed his forehead against hers. "Answer a question with a question. I really thought we'd moved past this stage, Kiley."

"You thought wrong. So?"

"If I tell you, will you tell me?"

"You go first this time."

"You are quick." Smiling, he drew in a deep breath.

"It's Jackson Pierce, it's a family name and if you laugh, I'll be forced to kill you."

The threat didn't appear to faze her, any more than a battalion had.

"Jackson Pierce." The first sputter escaped her.

"Kiley," he warned, tugging on her hair.

"Jackson Pierce." The sputter grew to a laugh.

"Kathleen!"

"Jackson Pierce." Her rich laughter spilled out.

Considering she was naked, J.P. found her quite a sight.

"Okay, Kiley, this is war." In a swift move that made Kat gasp, J.P. lunged, overbalancing them both onto the bed. Poised above her, expression triumphant now, he pinned her wrists over her head. "Now say you're sorry."

"I'd say it's a nice name." She bit her lip. "For a rich guy."

The green of her eyes gleamed in the pale moonlight, muted only by the fiery glow of her hair. *Fearless*, J.P. thought again. Even when overpowered and outgunned, Kat Kiley was fearless. "Do you ever give up, Kathleen?"

"Never, Jackson."

And somehow he believed her. "Neither do I," he murmured, "when I really, really want something."

Only in that moment did he know it was true.

And somehow in that moment, Kat believed him.

"I really have to go."

"I know." Though he released her wrists, he cupped her face instead.

At the abrupt change in tactics, Kat's heart thudded dangerously. She tried again. "It's late."

"You're right."

"You're not letting me up."

"That is a problem," he agreed.

For both of them. If there was a part of Kat that longed to escape, there was an equally strong, equally inexplicable force, that pulled her to stay.

As if sensing that vulnerable point, that small chink in her defenses, J.P. lowered his head inexorably toward her mouth.

"This is crazy," she murmured, in a last futile attempt at resistance. Even as she said it, however, her arms reached out to encircle his neck.

It *was* crazy. Had been crazy between them ever since the moment they'd met. And in that moment it was a craziness that seemed to rule them both.

Outside those doors, inevitably dark would turn into light and a generations-old war would continue to rage. But within that room, within that bed, there was only her and J.P. and war seemed very far away.

WHAT A DAY, J.P. thought later, much later, when he could think at all. *What a night.*

Despite the frenzied heat between them, J.P. felt curiously content, oddly at peace. Lazily, he reached out to stroke her bare back. Before he could touch her, Kat slithered off the bed.

Something about her hurried motions made J.P. sit up. Something about the way she hastily gathered her belongings made him frown slightly. He watched as she slipped on her T-shirt then her jeans, rapidly buttoning buttons—like a warrior donning armor, he thought, then frowned again at the analogy. "What's wrong?"

"Have you seen my other boot?"

"Kathleen?"

Something about his tone made her raise her head. Something about the look in J. P. Harrington's eyes made her glance away just as quickly. "Nothing. It's late, that's all."

"Actually," smiling slightly, J.P. glanced toward the window, "it's early."

So it was. As the first faint pink of dawn crept into the room, now it was Kat who frowned. It couldn't be morning. She never spent the night. "Oh, there it is."

Locating the other shoe, she jammed it on—as if she were drowning and it was a life preserver, J.P. thought. What had happened to all of Kat Kiley's fearlessness now?

"It's late," she repeated, already striding to the door.

"Hey, wait a minute."

"I have to go."

"I know, just give me a minute." Swinging his legs off the mattress, J.P. winced a little at the unexpected aches and pains. That's what you get for making love on the floor, he decided, as he searched for his own scattered clothes. But it was well worth it—she was well worth it. He located his shirt under the bed. "I'll walk you to your room."

That made Kat's backbone stiffen. Slowly, she turned. "I'm right next door, J.P., and I'm already dressed."

"Good." He put on his pants. "It'll be a short walk."

Muttering something about authority figures, Kat didn't stick around long enough to argue. Ignoring him, she marched out into the hall.

"Hey, wait a second." Abandoning his own search for boots, J.P. came after her barefoot. He caught her just as she was inserting her key into the lock. "You always were quick, Kathleen." Amused, he shook his head. "But aren't you forgetting something?"

"No." She twisted the knob.

"Not so fast." Before she could make her escape, he caught her by the shoulders, and whirled her around. "Good night to you, too," he murmured. Ignoring her struggles, he slanted his head to kiss her, then frowned.

"You know you never answered me. You're not involved with anyone, are you?"

Despite the situation, Kat had to laugh. "You and your questions, Harrington."

"You and your evasive tactics, Kiley." He caged her between his body and the wall. "And I should probably warn you right now, I'm not letting you go until you tell me."

She could have broken his hold. What pinned her was the steely determination in those gray eyes. "No, I'm not involved with anyone."

"Good."

That brought her head sharply round. "And I don't want to be, remember?"

"We'll see."

That quiet smile of J. P. Harrington's was maddening, Kat decided. Almost as maddening as his self-confidence. She might have dived into the fight, and she knew at least one part of her was itching to do exactly that.

Before she could, J.P. disarmed her completely. He just shook his head and lowered his mouth to hers.

Kat braced herself for the onslaught. Instead he merely brushed his lips against hers.

Caught off guard, she weakened and that was when he made his move.

He kissed her then, a kiss that was unlike anything they'd shared before. A kiss that was less about heat than it was about intimacy. A long, slow kiss that teased her senses with what could be, rather than what had been. It was not a kiss at all, Kat thought with rising panic, but a caress. And a promise of things to come.

Even as Kat reeled beneath it, J.P. abruptly released her. Eyes huge, she stared at him, suddenly grateful for the support of the wall.

Something J. P. Harrington seemed to know only too well. Kat found herself far less grateful for the pleased assurance in those gray eyes of his.

"Now, we've said good-night," he said quietly. "I'll wait until you get inside."

Still unsteady, Kat reached for the door. She stopped long enough to cast him one last appraising look. "You do fight dirty, Harrington." Then she disappeared into her room.

Inside, Kat paced. Sex, she reminded herself sternly, even great sex, was just that. A basic human need, a biological function and not to be confused with loftier emotions.

She wondered if their evening together had been a mistake. For a woman still sated with pleasure it was an odd thought. But J. P. Harrington had been far too smug about the whole thing. He might think he owned her soul, but no man, not even this one, would ever own her heart.

4

THERE WAS BARELY time for him to shower and shave before J.P. stood outside Kat's door. He knocked once, then again.

"Hey, Kat. Kathleen." She must have fallen asleep, and the thought of how she would look, how she would feel against him, made J.P. try the handle.

"Breaking and entering's a crime, mate, even in this country."

At the sound of Paul Collins's voice, J.P. spun around. He frowned as the Australian broke into a broad grin.

"Your girlfriend's downstairs and lookin' a damned sight better than you, if I may say so." Paul's grin grew even broader as his eyes took in J.P.'s appearance. "War's hell, eh, mate?"

"Shut up, Collins."

"Ah, now there's a blow from a man who's smiling. I'd ask how the evening went, but as you Yanks would say, a picture's worth a thousand words."

And a camera, J.P. thought with a sudden grin of his own, was worth even more. At least a certain woman's camera. He patted his bag with relish.

As the two men clattered down the stairs, Paul

stopped him at the entrance to the dining hall. "Just a friendly word of warning, mate. Press pool's going crazy."

J.P. lifted a brow. "How'm I doing?"

"Better than yesterday. 'Course that wouldn't be too hard."

Not as hard as entering that room. At J.P.'s entrance, the noisy clatter in the hall abruptly ceased. In unison, every head in the place swivelled between Kat and himself.

"Damn press," J.P. muttered.

Beside him, Paul chuckled, a chuckle J.P. might have shared if he hadn't noted something else.

At his entrance, every person in the room had looked up. That is, every person except one.

Across the far side of the room, a certain redhead suddenly seemed inordinately occupied with her gear. It might have been maidenly shyness that kept Kat's head averted. Then again, after last night, J.P. sincerely doubted maidenly shyness was one of Kat Kiley's problems.

He wondered what was. As he crossed the room, amid a nudging of elbows and even broader grins, J.P. had the distinct impression he was about to find out.

KEEP IT LIGHT, Kat reminded herself as she watched J.P. approach, *light and friendly*.

"Hi." He rolled to a stop right before her.

"Hi, yourself." But Kat couldn't quite bring herself to meet his eyes.

"So how are you?" J.P. murmured.

"Fine." She tossed her hair, hoping to appear casual. "How 'bout you?"

"A little tired, to tell you the truth."

So was she. And they both knew why. So much for light and friendly. It wasn't working any better than her decision not to spend the night. A little desperately now, Kat scanned the room, only to find Paul shepherding a reluctant press corps toward the door. "The truck is leaving," she muttered.

"I know." But when she started to move past him, J.P. blocked her path.

"Harrington—"

Tilting his head, he tried to peer into her eyes. "So, Kiley, are we supposed to be mad at each other or something?"

"I'm not mad."

"Good." But even as he angled his head to kiss her, Kat adroitly sidestepped him. "We have to go."

Exasperated, J.P. stared after her. "Hey." In two steps, he was by her side. "Hey, wait a minute." He put a hand on her shoulder, thinking to stop her.

At the light contact, Kat reared back.

Now J.P.'s eyes widened. "I thought you weren't mad."

"I'm not." But she could never seem to think when he touched her. That admission alone made Kat square off. "I am not mad," she repeated firmly. "And I'm not going to get into this now."

"Get into what?"

She raised her eyes to his face. "You're not going to let this go, are you?"

"You always were quick, Kiley."

Kat looked away. "Look, Harrington, I like you, all right, and last night was great, terrific, fantastic—"

"I agree. In fact, I could think of a few other adjectives."

"Don't!" She couldn't stop the sharp tone of fear in her voice.

He seemed to consider her for a moment. "All right," he said with a shrug, "we'll compromise. Let's just say I like you, too. So what seems to be our problem?"

"I told you." With difficulty, Kat controlled the edge that had crept into her voice. "I don't get involved."

"Really? Funny, that's not the way it felt to me last night."

No, it wasn't the way it had felt to Kat, either. But she had never liked being cornered. She found she liked it even less now. As always, with her back to the wall, she came out swinging. "Well, what are you waiting for, Harrington? Rave reviews? And here I thought you were little Mr. Security."

Beneath the attack, J.P. reeled. It wasn't just what Kat had said, it was the way she'd said it. Tough, cool. In that instant, Kat Kiley might have been a total stranger, a very hard stranger. Suddenly, last night seemed very far away.

Kat swallowed. "I don't want to hurt you, J.P. I really don't. But you're acting like we're a couple."

"And we're not? No, I guess we're not. Well then, what the hell are we?"

"I don't know." She ran a hand through her hair. "I don't know, all right? Two people who met and..."

"Had sex?"

"Yes. Yes, all right. We're two people who met and had sex. That's it, end of story. Is that what you were waiting for me to say?"

And here J.P. had always thought women were the romantic ones. As usual, Kat Kiley was teaching him differently. He drew in a long breath. "At least we both know where we stand."

Kat reached out to touch his sleeve. "I'm sorry, J.P., but I can't afford to get involved. I tried to tell you that last night. Nobody gets in the way of my work. Nobody. Not even you."

"But I'm not." Still not understanding, J.P. stubbornly shook his head. "I'm not getting in the way of your work."

"No?" Kat tossed her hair defiantly. "Then what are we doing in here, when we're supposed to be out there?"

She had a point. He had a better one. "What are you so afraid of, Kathleen?"

The simple question slashed through the quiet of the hotel, and with it, Kat's eyes flashed. "I am not afraid, Harrington."

In direct contrast to his quietness, she shouted, which was how J.P. knew he was right. "Yes you are, Kiley.

Only you're not afraid I'll get in the way of your work. You're afraid because you like me."

That little speech left her openmouthed. "As always, Harrington, your ego knows no bounds."

"Maybe, but I was in that room last night, too."

Now Kat's temper exploded. "God, you just think you have all the answers, don't you, Jackson Pierce Harrington? You think you have me all figured out. What did you do, take a pop-psychology course at Harvard?"

Yale, he might have corrected her. But then schools were not the issue. Nor was her work.

When he made no move to defend himself, Kat lost all interest in the fight. "I knew you wouldn't understand, Harrington. I don't know why I bothered. Now move. Move." She locked her eyes with his. "I have work to do."

"Fine." This time J.P. yielded her path. When she was several steps away, he added, "You...ah...might need this, Kathleen."

"Wrong again, Jackson." With a toss of her hair, she kept walking. "I don't happen to need anyone or anything."

"Really? That's a fascinating statement, coming from a combat photographer without a camera."

That stopped her cold. Her eyes flashed to her shoulder. Only then did she realize that her case wasn't on her arm. No, of course, it couldn't be. Because as she turned slowly she saw it in J. P. Harrington's hands.

Those gray eyes never wavered from her own. "You left it last night."

What he didn't say, what he didn't have to say, was that she'd left it after they'd... Kat swallowed hard.

For the first time in his life, J.P. didn't quite trust his temper around a woman. Rather than risk touching her, he tossed her the case. Even as she caught it, still Kat stared.

"You're welcome, Kiley."

No, J.P. thought, as he watched Kat wheel away, the war wasn't over yet.

OUTSIDE, Kat reached the press truck first. By the time J.P. caught up with her, she was already settled in a far corner where there was no room for him. By the small glint in her eye, he knew that was deliberate. J.P.'s jaw tightened.

Flopping down next to Paul Collins, J.P. immediately felt the Australian's gaze upon him.

"One word, Collins, one word about war and women, and I swear I'll hurt you."

"Not a peep from me, mate. Now Rogers here," Paul winked at the Brit, "he might give you a hard time. But I'm your friend."

"I'll say," the Englishman chortled. "He's got ten pounds wagered on you. And *he's* going to lose."

J.P. shook his head in disgust. "Don't you gentlemen have anything better to do with yourselves than to bet on my love life?" *Such as it was.*

"Not really, no." Rogers grinned.

"Not me, either," Paul agreed.

"Face it, Harrington," Rogers continued affably. "We're in this thing till the bitter end. And I'm going to win a lot of money."

"We'll see." Paul met the challenge with a grin.

As the press truck ground to a stop, J.P. and Kat jumped out at the same moment. Colliding, they found themselves nose to nose and toe to toe.

Even as J.P. reached out to steady her, his expression darkened. "Watch your butt out there, Kiley. The way I'm feeling right now, I'm not sure I'd save you today."

"That's perfect then, Harrington," came her ringing response, "because I don't happen to need saving from you or any man."

Behind them, J.P. heard the betting start up anew.

OUT ON THE BATTLEFIELD, cooler heads prevailed, as if both J.P. and Kat recognized that mere eye contact could raise the day's body count by at least one, possibly two.

At day's end, J.P. hurried back to his hotel room without a single backward glance and Kat Kiley did the same.

Fine, J.P. thought as he sat alone in his room, hearing Kat move around in her own. He had pride and he had principles on his side, not to mention the righteous fury of the unjustly accused. *I won't get in the way of your work, Kathleen. Just don't you get in the way of mine.*

Sitting down at the desk, J.P. punished his laptop, pounding out all his fury into his piece. And even he had to admit, twenty minutes later, he was pleased with the final result.

This story was undoubtedly the best he'd ever done. He knew he was a good journalist and he had a shelf full of awards to prove it. Yet if he'd ever received criticism, it was that he was too clinical, too detached. That was the age-old challenge of the foreign correspondent—to make readers feel as if they were there without letting the writer's own prejudices get in the way. In this piece, he knew he'd succeeded.

Calm now, J.P. tipped back in his chair to edit, when suddenly the door burst open. "Kat?" Hope sprang eternal.

He was trying to decide how cool to play it, when his face fell.

"Collins." J.P. shook his head. "Didn't your mother ever teach you to knock?"

"No, but she taught me to cover my butt. We're buggin' out, mate," the Australian announced dramatically. "Seems the guerrillas have overrun the joint. We're being evacuated. By helicopter, no less. Shades of 'Nam."

J.P. had no time to wonder that Paul seemed elated at the prospect. He grabbed for the bag containing his passport, then doubled back for his laptop and his story. No way was he losing all that heat.

Heat. Kiley. The association was instantaneous, as instantaneous as his instinct to save her.

Politeness abandoned, J.P. burst into her room. The sound of running water drew him to the bath. Without thinking, he thrust open the shower curtain...and stared.

"Harrington!" Outraged, Kat stared right back. "What the hell do you think you're doing?"

Unlike other women of his acquaintance, Kat seemed more angry than embarrassed. Then again, Kat Kiley had no reason to be embarrassed.

J.P. had always considered himself a rational, articulate man. Like his pride and his principles, it was one of his strengths. Yet in that moment, at the sight of Kat, wet, luscious and naked, J. P. Harrington couldn't seem to utter one single coherent, principled thought.

Kat had no such problem. "Listen, Harrington," she fumed. "We may have had sex together, but that doesn't give you the right to come busting in here—"

"Sex?" He raised his eyes to her face. "Is that honestly all you think it was? I told you I don't go around attacking women."

"Oh, that from a man who barges into my shower. And excuse me, but couldn't you find a better moment for a discussion about last night?"

Frustrated, irritated, J.P. ran a hand through his hair because, of course, she was right. This was neither the time nor the place.

"It was more than just sex." Grabbing her soap-slicked arm, J.P. yanked her from the tub. "But we'll fight about that later."

"Mind telling me what the hell is going on?" Even soaking wet, Kat blazed with anger.

"Not at all." He tossed her her jeans. "We're being evacuated."

J.P. had to hand it to her. Though her green eyes widened, Kat Kiley didn't need to be told twice.

Even as she threw on clothes, her second thought was for her work.

"Are you crazy?" J.P. shouted, watching in wild-eyed disbelief as she started to gather up photos and equipment and thrust them into her case.

"You know, I'm getting really tired of that particular question. And don't peek."

J.P. stared at her. "You are a very, very difficult woman to help, Kat Kiley."

"I know." Shutting the case with a little bang of finality, she grinned at him. "I'm also stubborn, rude, headstrong and have a few other character flaws I'm sure you've noticed and could comment on at length, but we are being evacuated. Maybe another time."

"I'll take a rain check."

"You could make a list." She hefted the case. "Thanks for coming for me, J.P." Kat put her hand in his. "Does this mean we're not mad at each other anymore?"

"No." He squeezed her fingers as they started to run. "And thanks for reminding me."

Hand in hand, they ran through the deserted hotel. As they burst out onto the street, the scene was one of bedlam. Everywhere the eye could see, there were people, people running and people screaming.

Only yesterday, Kat thought, the piazza had been a peaceful place, with children playing around the fountain and women chattering as they went about their chores.

But war was never very far away in this country.

Amid the chaos, Paul stood like a beacon, frantically waving his arms beside a waiting chopper.

As the blades sliced through air, they blew up waves of sun-scorched red clay. "Stay close," J.P. warned, tightening his grip.

"Like glue."

It was like running a human gauntlet.

"Grand adventure, eh, mates?" Paul yelled above the whirring blades.

As J.P. stared at the imperturbable Australian, he felt Kat let go of his hand and slip behind him. Whirling around, he caught her, camera poised, clicking away at the final vestiges of war.

"Goddamn it, Kiley!" The temper J. P. Harrington didn't know he had exploded. Grabbing her around the waist, he tossed her inside the chopper.

"You are a crazy woman," he stormed the instant he'd scrambled in after her.

Kat tossed her still-wet hair. "Thank you, Harrington."

And side by side, as the copter lifted off, they grinned at each other.

COMPARED TO WHERE they'd been, the international airport where they landed beckoned like an oasis of calm. As normal breathing returned, J.P. moved to help Kat out of the chopper, noticing too late she already was. "You okay?"

"Fine. In fact—" she patted her camera bag with relish "—I got some great shots."

J.P. scowled a little. "I guess I know that already, Kiley, since I was the one holding you on so you wouldn't fall out. You are not a dull date, I'll give you that." He tried to hold onto irritation, then lost that battle as well. Sighing, he tucked a lock of still-damp hair behind her ear. "Fortunately for you, you look good wet."

"And you, Mr. Harrington, look good shell-shocked." He did look good, Kat thought, with that small frown playing about his very determined jaw. Very good. So good, that giving into impulse, she reached out and drew his head near. "Thanks for saving me again," she whispered, her lips seeking his.

Kat had firmly intended to keep it light. That was before J.P. pulled her against him.

J. P. Harrington might be a gentleman, but he caught on fast. Then again, J.P. could never seem to remember that he *was* a gentleman where Kat was concerned.

He felt Kat's shock, her initial resistance and her fear, and deliberately he deepened the kiss. His instincts had been right—the response he sought bubbled there, right there under Kat's tough exterior. Vulnerable, she clung to him and J. P. Harrington hung on.

"Hey, mates, you could sell tickets to this event," Paul Collins said cheerfully as he approached.

Knowing the Australian was right, J.P. ended the

kiss. He kept his arms around Kat, however, knowing full well that if he didn't, she might have crumpled to the floor. So much for not getting involved, J.P. thought with a little smile.

"Well, I guess I've thanked you for saving me." Though her tone was light, she looked everywhere but at him.

"That's twice now, Kiley, I've gotten you to thank me. Careful, Kathleen, this is getting to be a habit."

"I have to find a phone," she muttered.

"What? I can't hear you."

At that, she pushed back. As she marched off, carried forward by that determined, almost military stride of hers, the two men watched her go.

"She's quite a woman, isn't she?" Beside him, Paul chuckled.

Yes, she certainly was. Even now, J.P. could scarcely breathe. Kat Kiley was a crazy, dangerous, unpredictable woman, a woman who made him think crazy, dangerous, unpredictable thoughts.

As PEOPLE BUSTLED around her, Kat hung on the line to New York. "Yeah, yeah that's right. A helicopter lift and everything. I got some terrific shots. Exclusives. *Where?*" she shouted above the din. "Where do you want me to go?" Unconsciously her eyes sought those of J. P. Harrington. Just as deliberately she looked away. "No, no problem. Yeah, I'll be there as soon as I can. No, I need the money."

Kat started to cross the concourse to tell him, but

something stopped her. She had warned him, she told herself, but even more, she had the feeling, the terrifying feeling that if she went back to him now she would never get away, never want to get away, again. No, this way was easier, easier on both of them. Penning a quick note, she found a porter.

"Excuse me, but do you speak English?"

"*Sí*. Yes." The dark-skinned man grinned.

"Then could you give this to that man over there? The one who looks like an L.L. Bean model."

"*Que?*"

"Sorry." She shook her head. "Just give this note to that man, okay?" When she slipped him several coins, he grinned. Kat did not smile in return.

Nor did J. P. Harrington when he read her note. At the simple salutation his heart tightened. It didn't get any better.

Dear Jackson:
I'm not a big believer in long goodbyes, so here goes: thanks for the memories and your good intentions, but you wouldn't want my soul even if you could have it. Catch you in the trenches.

Love,
Kat

P.S. Sorry I laughed. Jackson Pierce is a great name for a real gentleman.

Like Kat herself, her handwriting was bold and scrawled, and just like its author, the message was a mass of contradictions.

"The woman who gave you this?" J.P. asked urgently, glancing up. "Where is she?"

"Right there. By the *teléfono*."

But the space where Kat had been now stood empty. Just as abruptly, just as inexplicably as Kat Kiley had walked into his life, she'd walked right back out of it.

J.P. started to go after her, but something stopped him. Pride, yes, and principle, but something more: the cold, clear knowledge that nothing he said or did would make any difference. Even if he found her, she'd only run away again.

"Come on, mate," Paul urged with a hand on his arm. "I'll buy you a beer. You look like a man who could use one."

Unable to argue with that, the two men settled around a table. Tipping back his chair, Paul sighed. "Sheilas are a difficult lot, I'll give you that."

"Kat Kiley is a little more than difficult." If nothing else, J.P. still had his pride and he clung to it now. As if he couldn't care less, he crumpled the note into a tight ball and sent it sailing toward the trash.

When the missile missed its target by a country mile, Paul sighed again at the pitiful attempt.

"What are you supposed to do, Collins?" J.P. asked after a hefty slug of beer. "What are you supposed to do with a woman who warns you she'll hurt you and then does exactly that?"

"I don't know, mate." Paul called for a fresh round. "But I suppose it all comes down to just one thing."

"And what's that?"

"Is she worth it?"

As usual, the Australian was right. It was a question J.P. had no answer for. He thought of how Kat had looked bathed in moonlight. Of her teasing wit and how it made him smile. And then he thought of her angry defensiveness only this morning, as she'd fought him off. Angry, hurtful, wanting to hurt, and succeeding.

She was a study in contradictions. Flirtatious yet aloof, tough and yet somehow oddly vulnerable. A hard woman to care about, an even harder woman to understand.

Across from him, Paul held up his glass. "To war and to women."

But J.P. shook his head. "Who the hell are you, Kat Kiley?" he muttered. "Who the hell are you and what the hell are you so afraid of?"

5

RETURNING FROM A TRIP, Kat usually felt a certain sense of exhilaration, a residue of adrenaline. This homecoming, however, she felt only tired, and strangely out of sorts, which was stupid because the trip had gone very well, at least professionally. And that, she reminded herself sternly, was all she cared about.

Tossing down her bags, she surveyed her tiny apartment. The neighborhood was too far uptown to be considered fashionable...or even livable by most people's standards. The efficiency would have been empty had it not been for her photographs, which hung from every wall. A bunch of pictures—not much to show for her twenty-seven years on this earth.

She should get down to work now, she knew, but for once she couldn't muster up any energy or enthusiasm, and that thought alone was shocking enough to make her restlessly riffle through her mail. It was the usual assortment of unpaid bills, all except for one envelope that caught her eye.

Ripping it open, she stared at the message.

"The New York Press Club is pleased to announce your nomination for Best Newcomer award at a black-tie reception to be held..."

Kat didn't read any more. She didn't have to. This was a step forward, a big one. The New York Press Club was one of the most respected in the nation.

Hands trembling, still not believing, Kat scanned the note again, but this time she frowned.

A date. According to the invitation, she needed a date.

Unbidden, the face of J. P. Harrington flashed through her mind, a face she hadn't thought about, hadn't allowed herself to think about, since that fateful trip.

She must be tired. Before she could stop them, images of that night played through her mind. Images that made her smile.

No, Kat decided, tossing the invitation into her bag and grabbing her jacket. What she needed was a good dose of reality and Kat knew just where to find it.

IF SHE WAS GOOD at war, Kat had always thought, it was because she had grown up in a war zone. And this war, like all wars, claimed its victims.

As the train hurtled away from Manhattan, the topography visible through the window changed from the affluent luxury of New York and Connecticut's gold coast to the hardscrabble mill towns of the interior.

It was a part of the state most people didn't know existed. Lucky people.

Her hometown had changed little since Kat was a child. That was too bad. The brass factory still belched fumes into the leaden sky. Beneath its spirals, the people seemed all the more tired and gray.

The Kiley family homestead had changed even less over the years, and that was worse. Kat hurried past the overgrown yard choked with weeds, the sagging gate. Only in the kitchen was there any sense of life, or home.

Her mother worked at the sink, peeling potatoes with a practiced, weary hand. Francine Kiley, too, looked old, used up, Kat thought with a sudden pang to her heart, amazing for a woman only in her mid-forties.

Standing on the threshold, Kat tried to imagine the young woman, bright with promise, who had painted those watercolors locked away in the attic. The image refused to come.

But Kat loved her mother fiercely, even when Francine broke her heart, which was most of the time.

Her mother looked up then. Catching sight of her eldest daughter, she beamed, a proud smile that took years off her age. "Kathleen! Why didn't you tell me you were coming?"

"Because I wanted to surprise you." And surprise her she did. In a quick move, Kat grabbed her mother in her arms and whirled her around the room faster and faster until the older woman protested.

"Kathleen, stop. You're making me dizzy." But Francine laughed as she said it, pushing Kat into a chair. "I'll just fix you a plate. You're too thin."

Food was her mother's answer for everything, a panacea that had driven Kat crazy as a child. When her father would rage in his drunken stupor, cursing them all simply for being alive, her mother would clatter pots and pans. Either that, or run down to the church. Neither response ever solved a thing.

Bustling around the kitchen now, Francine served a plate of cookies. "So how was your trip?" Shaking her salt-and-pepper head, she paused at the refrigerator. "Imagine a child of mine in Central America."

"The trip was...okay." Kat didn't want to talk about it, because, as she reminded herself with a grimace, there was nothing to talk about. She took a bite of cookie.

"What's wrong?"

She caught her mother's worried eye. "Nothing. I'm fine, Ma. Just a little tired, that's all. Jet lag, I guess." She hadn't been very hungry lately, either, she realized, pushing the plate away.

"They're homemade!"

"I know."

"Kathleen, now I know something is wrong."

"Ma, I told you—"

"It's not right, Kathleen." Hovering over her like a mother hen, Francine clucked, "a young girl like you, all alone the way you are."

"I like to be alone. I need to be alone." Kat abandoned all pretense of eating now to stare her mother down. "And besides, Ma, you of all people should know that men don't solve problems." They only created them. And speaking of problems... "So, where is Jake, anyway?"

Kat refused, had always refused, to call him father.

That was a title that had to be earned, something Jake Kiley had never bothered to do.

Setting down a glass of milk, Francine's hand trembled slightly. "He's out. He had an errand."

"Another trip to McGeraghty's Bar and Grill, is what you mean." As both women knew well, milk was not exactly Jake's beverage of choice.

"Kathleen—"

"Why don't you leave him, Ma?" The words burst out of Kat fiercely, but then this was hardly unchartered territory between them. Even before her mother answered, Kat knew what she would say.

"I've made my bed, Kathleen. I've made my bed and I'll lie in it."

"What you made was a mistake. You got pregnant when you were seventeen years old, pregnant with me. Are you going to pay for that for the rest of your life?"

"Kathleen." Her mother turned her face away. "No more talk of this, please. It upsets me."

Because she saw it did, Kat let it go. Pick your battles, that was another lesson she'd learned early on. For Francine Kiley, religion was as much her salvation as it was her prison. It was pointless to argue. "I'm sorry, Ma." She reached across the table to squeeze her mother's thin hand, smiling slightly when her mother squeezed back.

"You scare me, Kathleen." Francine shook her head.

"Then I guess we're even, Ma. You terrify me."

As Francine dropped her hand, Kat changed the subject. "Well, Ma, guess what? I'm up for an award. The

New York Press Club thinks I just might be their most promising newcomer."

Francine blinked in disbelief, much the way Kat herself had done. With a laugh, Kat retrieved the invitation from her bag and shoved it into her mother's hands. "Here, I have proof."

As Francine scanned the thick sheaf, her hands trembled again, only this time for a different reason. "Oh, Kathleen, I just knew it. Knew if you could get away from this place your luck would change."

"Our luck," Kat corrected. "And speaking of which, since you're the one who gave me my first camera, I'd like you to come with me to the awards ceremony."

The light went out of her mother's eyes—as quickly, Kat thought, as it had come. Hurrying on, she pretended not to notice. "It's three weeks from now, and it's going to be in a big, fancy New York hotel. Tell you what, I'll even pop for a new dress for you and me. I think we deserve—"

"Kathleen, I don't think..." Francine sighed, began anew. "Kathleen, your father, he wouldn't like it."

Since Jake hadn't liked anything beyond the contents of a whiskey bottle for as long as Kat could remember, that hardly qualified as headline news. "Ma..." Though Kat Kiley rarely begged, this time she had to. "Ma, I need you there with me. Ma, I'm scared. Please."

"Oh, Kathleen—"

Just then there was a scuffle at the front door. Immediately, Francine was up on her feet. "You'd better go. Now, before he sees you."

If there was an irony in a child slipping out of the house before her own father could catch her, neither woman spoke of it—they were too used to it.

If it had been up to Kat alone, she would have stayed and fought, the same way she'd fought back when she was a kid. Nose-to-nose and head-to-head. Except she didn't have to pay the price for Jake Kiley's rages. Another person did.

At the back door, Francine stopped her with a hand on her arm. "Kathleen, are you sure you're all right?" The perceptive eyes of a mother scanned her child's face.

"Better than you." Kat cast a long, bitter look back toward the kitchen.

Every instinct within her screamed to grab her mother's hand and run, drag her away from this place as fast as they both could move. Except Kat knew her mother would never go.

"He'll sleep it off," Francine said quietly. "He always does."

"If he hurts you—"

Francine held her daughter's balled fist within one of her own. "Take good pictures."

That was the least she could do. That and one more thing. Reaching into her bag, Kat slipped several bills into her mother's resisting hand.

"Kathleen, no."

"Take it, Ma. Please, it will make me feel better."

With tears in her eyes, Francine gently touched her

eldest child's cheek. "You're a good girl, Kathleen Moira. You always have been, and you always will be."

HOME TWO WEEKS, and J. P. Harrington sat in his office, staring moodily out the window. From his vantage point, high atop Manhattan, J.P. should have seen a spectacular view of the city. Instead, he saw a Central American jungle and even more vividly, the light of the moon on...

Damn it. He swivelled around in his chair. He didn't have time for fantasies. What he needed was a date.

The New York Press Awards banquet, the journalistic social event of the season, loomed a mere three weeks away.

J.P. picked up the phone, then paused. He knew there were several women he could have asked. But there was only one woman he wanted to ask. The same woman he couldn't ask. And that fact made him scowl blackly.

It was a scowl his managing editor intercepted when he lumbered, not bothering to knock, into J.P.'s office. "Well, Harrington, you're up for another award."

"What?" Still glaring, J.P. looked up into Ed Lebar's face.

Through his bifocals, Ed glared right back. "That's supposed to be good news, Harrington."

"Oh." J.P. caught himself. "Oh, of course it is. I'm very pleased."

"So I see." Ed rolled his eyes. "Any more pleased, and we'll all be in trouble."

With a sigh, Ed dropped his bulk into a chair. "All right, Harrington, you know I'd rather walk over hot coals than have anything resembling a personal conversation, but I gotta ask. What the hell is eating you lately?"

J.P. blinked. "What do you mean?"

"What do you mean, what do I mean?" Ed swiped an impatient hand through his already messy gray hair. "I mean why are you going around looking like something that died yesterday only they forgot to tell you? You've been distracted, moody, irritable for weeks now."

"If you have a problem with my work..." J.P. began stiffly, but Ed held up a hand.

"I don't, and spare me the affronted-Connecticut-gentleman routine, Harrington, okay? Fact is, nobody's doing any work around this place lately. Stupid awards. No, I mean what's wrong with you? Not that I care or anything."

"Nothing's wrong, Ed." J.P. felt the beginnings of a reluctant smile twitch his lips. "At least, nothing around the paper."

"In other words, it's none of my damn business."

"I wouldn't have put it that way, but—"

"Right, right. You're a good reporter, Harrington."

"Thank—"

"A little soft sometimes, a little too kid-gloves for my taste, but good. Especially that piece you wrote from Central America. Now that had fire, punch. It grabbed a guy right in the gut."

Central America had grabbed him right in the gut, too, J.P. thought. "I was angry at the time," he said carefully.

Ed cocked a bushy brow. "You should get angry more often."

When J.P. said nothing, didn't know what to say, Ed heaved himself to his feet. "Got a date for the big shindig?"

"No."

"Me, neither."

"You're married."

"That's what I said, didn't I?" As J.P. smiled, Ed started for the door. "Oh, by the way," he tossed over his shoulder, "if I ever retire, although the world may come to an end first, I'd like you to take over as managing editor. And don't thank me, it's a crappy job."

As J.P. stared, Ed barreled out, practically knocking down the editor of the Style section in the process.

"Oh, good morning, Ed." Righting herself, Patrice Mansell's charm bracelet tinkled merrily. "I was just going to visit with J.P. here."

"Isn't anyone doing any work around this place?"

"Well..." As Ed lumbered off, Patrice stared after him. "He's in a bad mood."

"As always."

"And speaking of bad moods..." Patrice's eyes landed squarely upon him.

"I am not in a bad mood," J.P. defended himself. "I've been busy, that's all." As if to prove it, he industriously shuffled papers.

"You are a terrible liar, J. P. Harrington." She dropped gracefully into a chair. "You've been skulking around this place for weeks now. As a matter of fact—" a thoughtful look entered her blue eyes "—ever since that trip you took."

J.P. sighed. And here he'd thought he'd hidden it so well. "Aren't there any secrets around this place?"

"Of course not. It's a newspaper. And speaking of which, have you got a date yet for the press-awards dinner?"

"No!" And why did everyone keep rubbing salt in the wound?

"Good, because I came to ask if you wanted to go with me."

J.P. had to admit he never saw it coming. He looked up then, really seeing Patrice Mansell for the first time since she'd walked into his office. Even in a bad mood, he had to say it, she was easy to look at.

If anyone had asked him, he would have said he and Patrice were good friends, comfortable with each other. Elegant, refined, she was like the women he'd grown up with, like his own mother. And yet his judgment about women had been lousy lately. Very lousy. As if to prove it, he heard himself blurt, "Why? Why are you asking me?"

"Well," Patrice's soft laughter chimed delicately. "That certainly puts me in my place. And here I always considered you so well-mannered."

"I didn't mean—" J.P. still possessed sufficient grace to color. "I'm sorry. What I meant was, I thought you were dating that lawyer." That very successful corporate lawyer, if memory served. But then Patrice had been born to fish in big ponds.

"Chet and I...ancient history." She gave an indifferent wave of her hand. "He didn't want to get involved." Her expression darkened. "Feels a relationship would get in the way of his work."

J.P. felt a stab of instant sympathy. "Yes, there's a lot of that going around."

Her eyes lifted at that. "You, too?"

"Yes."

"Aha. Central America. I've got it...an exotic Latin beauty whose father has made a fortune in bananas but who disapproves of you, even if you are a catch, because you're not Catholic."

"No. A crazy American redhead who almost got me killed twice, made passionate love to me and then dumped me at an airport."

Patrice blinked. "Excuse me?"

J.P. sighed. "It's a long story."

"It wasn't that long a trip."

"Don't remind me."

"Well, J.P., what can I say? I hate her already."

At the memory of what she'd done, J.P. could almost hate Kat Kiley himself.

He looked up then to find Patrice's blue eyes upon him, a speculative gleam in them now. Miserably embarrassed at what he'd admitted, J.P. shifted in his chair. He must be comfortable with Patrice to have said all that. "I'd really appreciate it, Mansell, if you'd keep that story to yourself."

"The 'dump' or the 'passionate' part?"

She did know him well. "Both."

"You're right, they're equally out of character and I promise to keep both out of the Sunday society column."

"You're a pal."

Patrice winced at that. "Is the source of all this misery going to be at the banquet?"

J.P. nodded. "Yes. She's even up for an award." He'd heard that through the grapevine. As Patrice had pointed out, there were few secrets in the newspaper industry.

"Well." In one fluid motion, the editor rose to her feet. "They say misery loves company, J. P. Harrington. Would you care to join forces and be miserable together at the awards banquet?"

This time he didn't hesitate. "Patrice, I'd be honored."

Leaning on his desk, she quirked an elegant brow. "It promises to be an eventful evening."

"No," J.P. corrected, meeting her eyes. "It should be a hell of a night."

But then nights with Kat Kiley usually were.

6

On the eve of the banquet, Kat Kiley stood at the entrance to the elegant hotel ballroom, and immediately felt like a kid from the wrong side of the tracks.

She was unaccompanied and terrified. It was hardly an auspicious beginning to her first awards ceremony. But pride she had plenty of. It was pride that had made her splurge on this dress and it was pride that squared her shoulders now.

If only her stomach wasn't rolling in queasy tension, a sensation that increased a thousandfold when she spotted J. P. Harrington. Unlike herself, he looked right at home in these elegant surroundings. Like a man who'd been born to wear a tux.

Across the room, the collar of J. P. Harrington's tux suddenly felt as if it was choking him.

The woman he saw in that doorway was Kat Kiley, and yet it wasn't Kat at all. He might not even have recognized her, except for the unmistakable flame of her hair. Gone were the combat boots and jeans and in their place was a black velvet dress. It was a sleekly simple dress, a stunningly elegant dress. The high-necked bodice displayed a tantalizing hint of bare skin, and the narrow skirt molded her hips, taking its shape from the body beneath—the body he knew lay beneath from their one night of shared passion.

On another woman, it might have been severe, it might have been plain. Instead it was striking; *she* was striking. Unlike others around them, it was the woman who made the dress and not the other way around.

J.P. had thought her beautiful bathed in the light of the moon, he'd found her beautiful in combat gear, but nothing had prepared him for the sight of her now. Tonight, Kat Kiley looked both stunningly elegant and yet as sensual as sin.

Then again, that might have been his reaction to the wearer herself.

He wondered if she'd worn that dress deliberately to punish him; he wondered what she wore beneath it. Most of all, he wondered why he was wondering these things about a woman who'd made it clear she wanted nothing to do with him—a woman, J.P. reminded himself, he was angry at.

For long seconds, they stared at each other. In that moment, they might have been the only two people in the crowded room.

Beneath J.P.'s smoldering gaze, Kat shivered. His eyes swept over her body like a caress.

Except for the hint of temper in those cool gray eyes.

Even as Kat took an involuntary step toward him, deliberately, J. P. Harrington walked away.

If Kat hadn't been feeling well before, she felt much worse now. Taken aback, she stared after him, watching his stiff-backed stride as he disappeared into the crowd.

He was angry, Kat knew. Very angry. Well, she decided with a toss of her hair, there was certainly nothing new and different about that. She and J. P. Harrington had managed to get under each other's skin since the first moment they'd met.

It would have been a perfect moment to confide in a girlfriend. Except Kat didn't have a single friend to confide in. The truth was, J. P. Harrington, even in so brief a time, had gotten closer than most people ever did.

Alone, she wandered the room. She might be friendless, but Kat was honest, at least with herself. Somewhere between the appetizer table and the ladies' room, her basic sense of honesty compelled her to admit that if the situation had been different—if he had left her at the airport that way—she might have been angry herself. No, there was no *might* about it. She would have been furious, and, she concluded, hurt. If there was anything a kid from the wrong side of the tracks understood, it was the stinging wound of injured pride.

Kat squared her shoulders. It seemed she owed J. P. Harrington once again.

"IS THAT THE MISERY?" Patrice inquired of J.P.

Safe on the far side of the room, he nodded.

"That flashy-looking redhead in the too-tight dress?"

Too-tight dress? Flashy? Thinking they were speaking of two different women, J.P. turned. Kat had her back to him and now J.P. could clearly see what some kind god had spared him before.

For all its elegant front, her dress was nearly backless,

plunging to a deep V that revealed an ample expanse of silky flesh. Very silky flesh. Almost, but not quite as silky as the black sheen of her hose covering long legs, impossibly long legs accentuated by sexy, black strappy pumps.

Leave it to Kat Kiley and her infamous finales.

J.P. swallowed hard. It was going to be a long night. A very long night.

Over his shoulder, Patrice peered critically. "That style went out of fashion last year, you know."

But the body beneath it hadn't. And what bothered the editor of the Style section didn't appear to faze others in the least.

As Kat passed through the crowd, J.P. couldn't help but notice the way men's heads turned to follow her— even men who were clearly not alone.

He was not jealous, he told himself. No, he'd never been jealous about a woman in his entire life. That emotion was beneath him.

Murder, however, was not. If she didn't stop driving him to distraction...

"J.P.? J.P.!"

With difficulty he tore his glance away to meet another woman's eyes. Not green this time, but blue, cool blue with more than a hint of skepticism in them.

"I thought you hated her."

"I do. I *do*," he repeated more forcefully when Patrice raised a patrician brow.

"Then ignore her."

"That's exactly what I plan to do."

The editor did not look convinced. "Maybe I should play bodyguard."

"Patrice, please, I'm a big boy, and may I remind you, a seasoned combat veteran. I really think I can handle one redhead."

Feeling in need of a drink, a strong one this time, J.P. excused himself. He should have remembered that nothing to do with Kat Kiley ever turned out the way he'd planned.

Spotting J.P. alone at the bar, Kat made her move. Like a seasoned guerrilla fighter, she caught him unaware, and off guard.

"Hi," she murmured, suddenly appearing before him, right before him.

Startled, he stepped back.

J. P. Harrington was too well-bred to ignore a woman completely. Still, he managed to make his point. Nodding his head, he murmured a cool, "Good evening." His tone could have chilled an ice cube. "I didn't notice you come in."

"Right, Harrington." Before him, Kat rolled her eyes. "My skin is still blistering from your not noticing."

"Well, Kiley, isn't it fortunate for both of us then that you're tough?" He looked past her. "Now, if you'll excuse me..."

When he would have moved on, she stopped him.

"You're mad," Kat said from behind.

He paused in midstride. "You're quick."

"You're mad because I left."

Not that quick. He spun around to face her. "No, I'm mad because of the way you left."

Seeing the fury in those normally quiet gray eyes now, Kat took a step back. Though she told herself she couldn't care less what he thought of her, the problem was, she did. "I...I left you a note."

"Yes, I got it. Thank you, I'll cherish it forever."

The sarcasm stung. He was not a man to take easily or lightly, Kat was reminded again. Even in a tux, J. P. Harrington looked like he could go a few rounds.

The only problem was, tonight she couldn't, not the way she felt.

"Look, Harrington...in case you haven't gotten it yet, this is my way of apologizing. Oh, forget it." At his suddenly blank expression, her stomach lurched alarmingly.

Because it was a choice between passing out or sitting down, Kat chose the latter.

J. P. Harrington blinked. As usual, one minute Kat was there and the next, gone. He might have walked off forever, except that last little speech of hers had made him curious. Curious enough to make him tempt fate again. Cautious now, like a man expecting a live grenade to blow up in his face at any minute, J.P. approached.

"As always, Kiley, you have an interesting way of ending things."

"Thank you. I'll take that as a compliment." She kept her head averted.

"And as I've always said, you're an unusual

woman." He stared down at her bright red hair, noting almost despite himself the shades within shades accentuated by the ambient light. "But I thought you never apologized."

"I don't." That had her head up. "You're catching me in a weak moment."

Yes, J.P. saw he had. Only now did he see what she hadn't let him see before. Her hair might entice his hands, her dress might attack his nervous system, but Kat Kiley was so pale her freckles stood out. So pale he forgot to be angry. "You're sick."

"You're pretty quick yourself, Harrington. But I'm not sick." She waved an irritated hand. "I am never sick."

Staring down at her pallor, he was forced to disagree. "Oh, I believe you. But I think your stomach might have doubts."

Kat smiled a little at that. "It must be jet lag."

"It can be a killer. How long have you been back?"

Almost three weeks, Kat thought with a frown. Too long to be feeling so bad. "Maybe it's nerves."

"Nerves? You?" J.P. laughed. "Excuse me, Kiley, but a woman who almost got us both mowed down by a battalion for a couple of photographs is not going to get nervous over a simple award."

When Kat's eyes shot up, suddenly J.P. stopped laughing. Only then did he realize what he'd admitted, what she'd admitted as well with that look. No, he thought, neither one of them had forgotten that night in Central America, no matter how hard either of them might have tried. And in that moment, he further suspected that Kat had tried to erase that memory even harder than he.

This was complicated, J.P. decided, very complicated. And being a man who played it safe, this time it was he who retreated. "Maybe a drink would help?"

"Thanks." Kat nodded.

"Tonic water, right?"

The instant J.P. approached the bar, Patrice appeared at his side. This seemed to be his night for being ambushed. "I thought you were going to ignore her."

"I am. I will." Under the editor's steady gaze, he lost his last line of defense. "What do you want me to do, Patrice? She's not feeling well."

"You're not looking too steady yourself." Drink in hand, she pivoted gracefully to pick out a figure in the crowd. "You know, it's funny, she doesn't strike me as your type."

"I'm not sure she is. I'm not sure Kat Kiley wants to be any man's type."

"Then why punish yourself?"

"I don't know."

Unfortunately, the answer didn't get any clearer. Making his way back to Kat's side, J.P. handed her the drink. "Feel better?"

"Better" was a relative term. Even feeling lousy, Kat was quick, quick enough to catch that touching scene by the bar. She wondered why J. P. Harrington was so mad—he'd certainly landed on his feet. And then she wondered why she cared. She told herself she didn't, which, of course, did little to explain her own anger. "I'm fine, Harrington, and that's more than I can say for your girlfriend over there."

He raised a brow. "Girlfriend?"

"Yeah, the icy stick giving me the evil eye, even as we speak."

Following the direction of her gaze, J.P. turned. Patrice Mansell was certainly not an icy stick, nor was she giving them the evil eye, but there was a coolly appraising light in her gaze.

It was funny, really. Of the two women, Patrice was the more classically beautiful. If the editor was all refinement and style, then Kat Kiley was all edges, edgy attitude and even edgier eyes. And yet J.P. had no trouble turning back, even if he did repeatedly get bruised by those edges. "She isn't my—"

"Is she rich, too, Harrington? Of course, she is. Hope her money's worth it. She looks like she's got a nasty temper to me."

Personally, J.P. thought the description more aptly fit another woman in that room. But if Kat's arch tone surprised him, there was still a part of J. P. Harrington that was human enough to make her want to suffer a little—payback both for leaving him and the vicious attack of that dress on his nervous system. "Taste is a relative thing," he informed her smoothly.

"Obviously." Over his shoulder, Kat answered Patrice's icy look with a scorching glance of her own.

Before war could erupt, J.P. shifted, blocking her view. "So, Kiley, which one of these gentlemen is your date? Let me guess. The earringed stud over there—now, he looks like he could stop a tank with his bare hands."

"Ha, Harrington! That just goes to show that while you may think you know everything, you don't. It so happens I don't have a date."

"No? And why not? Not for lack of offers, I'm sure. Not the way you look in that dress."

J.P. could have flogged himself for that. For once Kat didn't seem to notice.

Her airy tone disappeared. "Because I got stood up. I got stood up by my own mother."

Had she really thought that Francine would finally start fighting back, now? Yeah, that's exactly what she'd thought, hoped. Which just went to prove what an idiot she was. Francine would never fight back, not even for her daughter. After twenty-seven years, Kat knew she shouldn't be surprised. Of course, after twenty-seven years, it still shouldn't hurt.

Above her, J. P. Harrington forgot to wonder what Kat Kiley had on under that dress. He was too busy wondering at the pain on her face.

He hadn't meant to hit a nerve, but the truth was, despite what they'd shared, he still didn't know her very well. "I'm sorry, Kat."

"I *must* be sick," she muttered. "You didn't even have to pry that out of me." She looked up then. "And I didn't tell you that to make you feel sorry for me, Harrington."

Now Kat Kiley's pride registered as well. At least, J.P.

thought, he could give her that. "Kiley," he said lightly, "it's difficult to feel sorry for a woman who looks the way you do tonight."

"Really?" She tilted her head and her eyes danced a little.

Almost unconsciously, J.P.'s glance strayed over the velvety skin of her bare shoulders. Try as he might, he couldn't help but remember the night he'd kissed that skin, caressed it, tasted it.... Aware of her scrutiny, he raised his eyes back to her face. "Well, let's just say, if you looked any better I'd be a dead man."

"You probably will be very soon, Harrington." Rising, Kat cast a pointed look in Patrice's direction. "I don't think your girfriend's any too happy with you." Kat turned to leave.

"She isn't my girlfriend," J.P. said quietly, from behind her.

"Oh?" Despite herself, Kat swung back.

"No." He shook his head. "She's just a friend."

"Really? Are you sure she knows that?"

With her arched brow, Kat still looked beautiful...and just as skeptical as Patrice Mansell had before. "Would you like her to come over and corroborate my story?"

"Not necessary, Harrington." She gave an airy wave of her hand. "Your life is none of my business."

Before J.P. could frame a suitable retort, around them the lights dimmed—a signal that the awards ceremony was about to begin. "I think that's our cue to find our seats," Kat murmured.

It might not have been any of his business, but as Kat scanned the crowd, J.P. couldn't help but think that she looked a little lost. "Do you...ah...know anyone here? Because you can join us, if you'd like."

"I doubt your girlfriend would appreciate that."

"I told you, she isn't my—"

"Oh, look, there's Sammy and some of the other stringers. I think I'll join them. Good luck, Harrington."

"Yes, you too, but she isn't my—"

"And do me a favor," Kat tossed over her shoulder, already on the move. "Tell your girlfriend to keep her evil eyes off me." She smiled sweetly. "I wouldn't want to have to scratch them out for her." On that note, she sailed off.

Staring after her, J.P. could only shake his head and smile.

Still, he had to admit he was more than a little relieved that Kat hadn't joined them. As their last encounter had proven only too well, the situation between himself and Kat was complicated. His own feelings toward her were complicated. Then again, the whole evening was complicated and getting more so by the minute.

As J.P. murmured his hellos to Ed Lebar and his wife, he took his seat next to Patrice. Immediately, he felt the blonde's cool eyes upon him.

"How's your girlfriend?" she murmured.

"She sends her regards."

"I'll bet."

To smooth his date's ruffled feathers, he gave gallantry a try. "Have I told you yet tonight, Patrice, how lovely you look in that dress?"

She held up a hand in front of his eyes. "What color is it?"

"Ah..."

"Don't even try to lie, J.P." When she sighed, her blond page boy swung. "And don't say another word. You're already in trouble."

He suspected she was right, there. When the newcomer category, Kat's category, was announced, he glanced over to where the redhead sat.

He supposed most people would never guess how nervous she was, but he could, by the way she squared her shoulders. He was surprised to find his own palms a little sweaty.

"And the winner is..."

Come on, J.P. thought. *Give her this.*

"Kat Kiley! UPI."

"Yes!" Like a shot, fist clenched in victory, J.P. was out of his chair.

He hadn't intended to do that. Nor to be quite so obvious. Very obvious, given the way Kat looked at him as she made her way to the stage. As she found his eyes, a small smile played around her lips.

A smile that made J.P. fall back in his chair. Suddenly he was aware that everyone around the table was staring at him.

It was Ed, never a man known for his tact or interpersonal skills, who put the question into words.

"Why are we so happy all of a sudden?" the managing editor blurted. "Do we know this person?"

"Only in the biblical sense," Patrice muttered under her breath.

"What?" Ed glared at his wife. "Why are you kicking me? The guy's looked like he's been dead for weeks now and suddenly he's turning cartwheels over some redhead we don't even know? And you don't think I should even ask?"

But J.P. barely heard them. All his attention was riveted on a certain woman on the podium. Eyes shining, Kat gave her acceptance speech, a beautiful, sexy redhead in a daring gown. Standing there, she looked every inch the confident winner.

And yet, she was all alone, he knew. All alone for her first award. That got to him.

Kat had come without a date by choice, J.P. reminded himself. Hadn't she made that abundantly clear? And yet, remembering her expression when she'd told him about her mother, he wondered what that was all about as well. Even later, when he won in his category, the thought of Kat Kiley lingered in his mind.

As the ceremonies wound down, the well-wishers gathered around. He could have gone to her then, J.P. thought. Could have congratulated her. It would have been the perfect excuse.

And yet, he hesitated. He wasn't sure living dangerously agreed with him. Then again, he wasn't sure playing it safe had made him feel any better. She was complicated, very complicated. And did he need complications in his life?

But the real stopper was that Kat Kiley had hurt him, hurt him too badly to risk taking a chance again. Confused, he sought out Patrice's advice.

The move was not lost on Kat Kiley. She watched their fair heads bent together. *A perfect match*, she thought and was surprised by how much that hurt, how strange that made her feel. But then she'd been feeling strange for weeks now. Ever since that damned trip, ever since she'd met him. Very strange.

And even as J.P. was taking his emotional temperature, Kat made up both their minds.

"Well, Harrington," Patrice murmured, "aren't you going to make your move?"

"I don't know. I'm thinking it over."

"Well, you'd better think fast," she advised, gazing over his shoulder. "She's leaving."

"Excuse me?"

"Your girlfriend? The misery? She's leaving even as we speak."

"What?" J.P. forgot to be polite.

"Look for yourself, Harrington."

He turned, and there indeed was Kat Kiley, heading for that door. At the sight, J. P. Harrington narrowed his eyes in determination. *No*, he thought, *no, not this time.* This time, he was going to do the ending.

Before he could think better of it, before coolheadedness and logic could prevail, J. P. Harrington was across that room.

"What, Kiley, no note this time?"

Caught off guard, Kat whirled around to defend herself. The quick move proved a fatal error in tactics. That strange feeling she'd been battling for weeks now erupted into a full-scale attack of dizzying nausea. Suddenly, J. P. Harrington's face blurred like a lens out of focus. Before she could stop herself, before she could prevent it, she felt herself falling...falling.

Sheer instinct made him reach out. Before she could crumple to the floor, J.P. caught her.

Astonished, he stared down at the redhead in his arms. He noticed several other people staring at them as well.

Kat Kiley was definitely not a predictable woman.

Because he didn't know what else to do with her, he guided her into a chair. "Kat? Kathleen?"

"Oh, God." She looked up into J. P. Harrington's face. His very concerned face. "Thanks."

"You're welcome."

"Feel better?"

"Mind if we save the questions for later?" As a fresh bout of nausea overcame her, Kat bolted from the chair.

J.P. grabbed her arm. "Wait a minute, Kiley. Where the hell do you think you're going now?"

"To the ladies' room. I'm going to be sick."

"What?"

Kat pushed against him. "Move, Harrington, move! Move or I'll throw up all over your tux."

Because her pea green complexion told him she was right, J.P. reared back, hands raised. He watched Kat

Kiley hurtle toward the ladies' room. She had always been quick, he thought.

It was unfortunate that Patrice Mansell chose that exact moment to stroll over. "So, how's your girlfriend?"

"Ah...fine." Casting a worried eye in the direction Kat had fled, he only hoped that was true.

"Is that why she did the fifty-yard dash to the ladies' room, the color of an avocado?" Surveying him, she shook her head.

Patrice was right—there truly were no secrets in the newspaper business. "Look, maybe you could go in after her?"

At the very suggestion, Patrice backed away. "Oh, no, Harrington. Oh, no, maybe *you* are into punishment, but you're not dragging me into all this."

"Patrice, please."

"Harrington, now why would I help her? I don't even know her. And besides, I sincerely doubt if she's going to thank me."

In that instant J. P. Harrington knew exactly how Patrice Mansell felt. No, Kat would never thank them. "For me," he coaxed, "and because she really needs the help."

"Right, Harrington, go for the low blow."

"Patrice—"

"Fine, I'll do it, but you owe me. You owe me big time."

WITH HER HEAD hanging over a toilet bowl, the last person Kat Kiley expected or wanted to see was the frosty blonde who'd been looking daggers at her all evening.

"Excuse me," the blonde said coolly. "I don't believe we've met. I'm Patrice Mansell."

"Yeah, well...you'll forgive me if I don't shake."

In a single glance, Patrice took in the situation. "I'll go get J.P."

That had Kat rising up, or at least trying to. "No."

The blonde stopped. "Look, Ms. Kiley, we don't know each other, and I suspect even if we did, we wouldn't like each other very much, so I'll be blunt—it's ridiculous, not to mention childish to refuse help when you so obviously need it. Now, I'll go get J.P."

With that, Patrice swept toward the door on high-heeled pumps.

The woman knew how to get even. In her wake, a cloud of perfume drifted. At the cloying scent, Kat turned green and hastily sank back to her knees. *And to think,* Kat fumed weakly, *I used to beat up girls like that when I was a kid.* She hated being sick.

"YOU'D BETTER GO in there," Patrice told J.P., who was hovering right outside the door. "You were right. She needs help."

When he would have dashed off, the editor caught his sleeve. "A word of warning, friend. She's not going to thank you, either."

Nobody knew that better than J. P. Harrington.

"And to think," Patrice said with a sigh, "you were supposed to be my date tonight."

"To think." Giving in to impulse, J.P. stopped long enough to brush her check with a kiss. A very brotherly kiss. "You're one nice lady, Mansell."

"Nice guys finish last," she called after him.

KAT KILEY WAS the first woman J.P. had ever braved a battalion for, and she was certainly the first to get him inside a girls' bathroom. Of the two, the latter was the act of infinitely greater valor.

Squaring his shoulders, J.P. marched in. He found her in the last stall. Just as Patrice had predicted, she looked none too happy to see him.

"Are you crazy?" Kat gasped. "You can't come in here."

Then again, she was in no shape to put up much of a fight. Even forewarned, still J.P. wasn't prepared for her alarming pallor.

"Kat? Kat, are you all right?"

She shot him a look, and even J.P. had to admit it was a stupid question to have asked of a woman in an evening gown kneeling on a bathroom floor.

But when he started to approach, Kat held up her hand. "No, no, I'm fine."

"Yes, I can see that."

Fighting valiantly, she rose to her feet, but at the effort she swayed dizzily on her heels. Instantly, J.P. was at her side. "Okay, Kathleen, come on, let's go."

"I told you I don't need any help." She batted at his hands. "Only one Victorian swoon for the evening, Harrington, I promise."

Since she was showing a lot of the old fight, J.P. released her. Nonetheless, he stood right behind just in case.

It galled Kat that she had to hold on to the wall to make it to a chair. Then again, it was better than meeting J. P. Harrington's eyes. Or having him touch her again.

By the time she reached the lounge area of the bathroom, she felt as though she'd run an obstacle course. To hold herself upright, she was forced to lean heavily against a counter. Still, old habits died hard. "Well, Harrington, you asked what I did for my finale?"

"Very intriguing," he agreed.

In the mirror, their eyes met. It was Kat who broke their gaze first. "Thanks for your help, J.P."

"No problem."

"There might be a small one." Kat drew in a shaky breath. "You're still in the ladies' room."

"I know." In the mirror, she watched as he shifted uneasily, more than a hint of color spreading over his own face now. "But I was worried."

Yes, she could see he was, and at that, coupled with his embarrassment, something caught in Kat's heart. "Maybe you should leave."

He didn't need to be asked twice. Obviously relieved, he virtually sprinted to the door. But even with his hand on the knob, he paused. "I'll be right outside, if you need me...."

The problem was, Kat thought as the door snicked shut, leaving her alone again, that she didn't want to need anyone. *Didn't* need anyone, she corrected herself firmly. That from a woman who was forced to lean on the sink just to wash her face and hands.

And for a woman who had never needed anyone, had never wanted to need anyone, Kat was inordinately happy to see J. P. Harrington's tall form striding toward her the minute she exited the bathroom. Even if she couldn't quite meet his eyes.

"How do you feel?"

"Better." Kat tried to toss her hair. This time, the gesture obviously didn't fool anyone, not even herself. "Tired but better."

"Good." He slung on his coat. "I'll drive you home."

"J.P., that really isn't—"

He rounded on her furiously. "Kiley, if you think I'm leaving a woman all alone in the middle of New York City, dressed the way you are and sick to boot, then you really are crazy."

With that, he firmly took her arm in his and escorted her toward the door.

Beside him, Kat Kiley could only blink. *J. P. Harrington was tough*, she thought. *Maybe as tough as she was. Maybe even tougher.*

7

OUTSIDE, the February night was frigid, as bitterly cold as the Central American jungle had been hot.

There was no middle ground between him and Kat Kiley, J.P. thought. So why the hell did he have his arm around her, holding her close?

This time, the answer came readily enough—because if he didn't, she would have toppled to the ground. Just as she had in that airport, she clung to him, not with passion this time, but vulnerability.

As he handed the valet his parking ticket, Kat shivered. Against his side, he felt rather than saw the tremors and frowned down. "I think we forgot your wrap, Kat."

"My what?"

"Your coat, Kiley." His breath came out in a frosty whoosh. "Damn it, Kathleen, it's twenty degrees out here. No wonder you're sick."

At any other time, he was sure Kat would have dived into the fight. This time her words came out muffled against his chest. "I don't happen to have a wrap, Harrington, and I didn't think a flak jacket would work with this dress."

Even as he shook his head, J.P. shrugged out of his

own coat. "You don't need a lover, Kiley, what you need is a keeper."

"Are you volunteering?"

More like he'd been volunteered. He wrapped the heavy Chesterfield around her. Through the darkness of the night, he caught the deep green of her eyes. Holding her by the lapels of his own garment, he tugged until her nose was mere inches from his own. "One word, Kiley, one word, about my saving you again and I swear I'm taking it back."

"Actually—" she snuggled into the sudden warmth, realizing only then just how cold she'd been "—I was going to thank you."

"Thank me?" When her teeth chattered again, he wrapped his arms around her, turning her to rest his head against the bright fall of her hair. "You *must* be sick."

He realized how sick as the valet brought around his car, a 1966 MGB convertible in deep forest green, restored to a fare-thee-well. That car was his pride and joy—a rich man's extravagance, he knew. But when Kat made no comment, when nary a teasing remark passed through those lips, J.P. knew she was feeling really bad.

As he held open the passenger side door, she flopped into the seat and closed her eyes.

Taking his place behind the wheel, J.P. switched on the ignition, then turned the heater on full blast. "Where do you live? Kat? Kathleen?"

Beside him, Kat Kiley slumbered on. Even when he gently nudged her shoulder, she barely stirred.

J.P. supposed he could rifle through her bag and find her address. Even crazy women undoubtedly carried identification. Except he made the mistake of looking at her then, really looking at her.

Snuggled in his oversize coat, her wild mass of hair tumbled askew, her cheek resting against the seat and her eyes closed, she didn't look like a woman who'd almost gotten him killed twice, nor the same woman who'd dumped him at the airport. In that instant, Kat Kiley looked about ten years old.

And very, very appealing.

Live dangerously. On that thought, J.P. turned the little roadster in the direction of his own apartment.

During the entire trip across town Kat didn't move, not even when he parked the car and opened the passenger side door.

"Okay, Kiley, rise and shine." Taking her by the arm, he tried to slide her out, but when that didn't work, he simply lifted her and carried her into the building.

It was the kind of posh address that, under ordinary circumstances, would have made Kat laugh. The kind of address that frowned upon unconscious women being carried into the lobby. At the sight of J.P., or more precisely J.P. and company, the doorman gaped.

"Good evening, Mr.—Mr. Harrington?"

"Hi, Charlie. Chilly tonight, isn't it?" When the doorman still stared, J.P. shifted Kat slightly in his arms. It didn't look any better, but at least now her head didn't droop. "She's not feeling well," he explained.

"Is..." The little man inched forward. "Is she breathing?"

"Oh, she's fine. It's the rest of us I'm worried about. Could you get the elevator for me?" With his chin, J.P. pointed to the button.

"Oh...oh, certainly, sir."

Right, J.P. thought. And there'd undoubtedly be a note in his box from the building's board of directors in the morning. "Dear Mr. Harrington, though your credit is beyond reproach, we must question your actions on the evening of February 9th."

In front of his door, he struggled for the keys deep in his pocket. That was no easy feat, given the woman in his arms.

Come on, Kiley, for once in our relationship, could you help me? But when he tried to set her down, Kat flopped like a rag doll.

Fine, Kathleen, we'll do this your way. The hard way. Holding her in one arm, he managed to snag the key, hit the lock and swing the door open all in one fluid motion.

He kicked it shut behind him, rather pleased with himself. Until he remembered the last time he'd done exactly that.

Inside his apartment, he hesitated. Bed or couch? *What the hell, if you're going to live dangerously you might as well go all the way.* Striding into the master bedroom, he laid her down on the bed.

She didn't even stir. Looking down at her, J.P. considered calling a doctor, but decided her color was better.

Much better. Just to make sure, he checked—she was still breathing.

Removing his coat from her shoulders, he tossed it aside. Her black pumps soon followed. And then J.P. hesitated.

It was a beautiful dress, far too beautiful to ruin by sleeping in it. Determined, he struggled with the side zipper. Somehow, in the delicate maneuver, his hand accidently brushed against the fullness of her breast. Her breast covered in warm, silky velvet.

His hand dropped away as if he'd discovered a ticking time bomb. Then again, maybe he had.

If he'd needed a reminder that Kat Kiley was no helpless ten-year-old, that was it.

Hastily, he zipped her back up. Then, just for good measure, he carefully pulled the spread over her and snuggled it up to her chin.

Feeling safer now, he retreated to the bathroom. He changed out of his tux into sweatpants and shirt, and when he came back out, Kat had curled onto one side. She was cozily oblivious in sleep.

J.P. wished he could do the same. He realized only then how often over the last five weeks he'd imagined Kat Kiley in that bed, in his bed. Of course, he admitted ruefully, in his fantasies, she hadn't been unconscious at the time. Then again, nothing with her had ever gone the way he'd planned. He certainly couldn't have anticipated this finale. Neither, he imagined, could she.

Settling in a chair, J.P. watched her. *Who the hell are*

you, Kat Kiley? he wondered. *And what the hell am I supposed to do with you now?*

WHEN KAT AWOKE the following morning the first thing she saw was J. P. Harrington's face. He was fast asleep, propped in a chair, a chair that was far too small for his tall frame.

And just the sight of him made Kat smile.

As if feeling it, J.P. awoke, yawning.

"Hi," she murmured as his lids drifted open.

"Hi, yourself." He winced as he stretched his neck. "How do you feel?"

"Fine." Kat blinked. "What are you doing here?"

"No, Kiley, sorry. The question you should have asked is 'What am I doing here?'"

Glancing around the unfamiliar room, Kat decided he was right. "Just out of idle curiosity, where the hell am I?"

"My apartment." Her gaze completed another circuit of the room landing on his face. J.P. was struggling against a smile. "I...ah...didn't know what else to do with you last night."

"What happened? No..." Kat held up a hand. "No, don't answer that." With horrifying clarity, the events of the previous evening danced through her mind. "Oh, God." She buried her face in her hands.

Like a flash, he was out of the chair. "Are you going to be sick again?"

"No, just mortified. Did I really almost throw up on you and then pass out?"

"Do you really want me to answer that?" Giving in to the urge to smile, J.P. settled on the edge of the mattress. He watched as Kat shook her head in stunned disbelief.

"I am never sick. Never. It must have been that chicken."

"I don't think so. You were sick even before you ate. Besides, I had it. So did everyone else in that room."

"Thank you so much for pointing that out, Harrington."

"Anytime. Think of it this way, Kiley, at least you got some sleep."

Her head shot up at that. "You're really enjoying this, aren't you?"

"Immensely." That was nothing short of the truth.

Kat Kiley wasn't pale now. She was bright pink, a vivid shade that clashed with her hair. From his vantage point, J.P. wondered if she knew how beautiful she looked when she was vulnerable, when she allowed herself to be vulnerable. It wasn't a view, he imagined, most people got to see.

With nervous fingers, Kat pleated the sheets. "Looks like I owe you again, Harrington."

"Looks like it." He matched her tone for casualness. Though nothing else was clear, he had already decided one thing: he wasn't going to make it easy on her. Not this time.

She met his eyes. "Well, I've lost my soul, I'm fresh out of cash and now it seems I've managed to misplace my dignity as well. I'm not really sure what I have left to offer."

Repressing his own ideas on that subject, J.P. rose from the bed. "Maybe you'll think better over some coffee. Think your stomach can handle it?"

When she nodded, he started for the door. "The bath is through there." He pointed. "Help yourself to a shower if you want. There are some fresh towels in the linen closet."

"Thanks. You're being incredibly nice about this."

"Incredibly," he agreed.

Though her face flamed, Kat kept going. "While we're at it, Harrington, I probably owe your girlfriend an apology as well. I don't think she liked me."

At the door J.P. stopped and turned. "For the last time, Kiley, Patrice Mansell is not my girlfriend. She's a friend who's a girl." He reached for the handle. "Oh, and while we're at it, you'll notice that you're still dressed. I told you I don't go around attacking women."

The instant he left, Kat fell back on the bed and hid her now scarlet face in her hands. For a woman who didn't need anyone, she'd certainly made a mess out of things.

Well, it was too late to do anything about it now. She could scarcely hide out in his bedroom all day. Besides, hiding out had never been her style.

Cautious now, Kat rose from the bed. When the room didn't tilt crazily, she knew she was fine.

A bug, she decided. One of those twenty-four-hour things. She felt good as new.

Which was more than she could say for her dress.

Glancing down at herself, she groaned. She looked like a woman who had slept in her clothes.

At least that was something she could fix. She made her way into the bathroom—a very nice bathroom, very tasteful, just like the bedroom. And well stocked. She fingered the rich texture of a thickly woven towel.

Well, if she had to throw up on somebody, she'd certainly chosen well. Feeling grungy in these elegant surroundings, she decided to take J.P. up on his offer. Stripping off her crumpled dress, she climbed into the shower. Ah, hot water. Now there was a luxury.

Several minutes later she heard a soft knock on the door. "Hey, are you all right in there?"

"Fine." Kat switched off the water. "Why? We're not being evacuated again, are we?"

"No. Not this time."

Even through the barrier of wood, she heard his light laugh. "Good, I'll be right out."

"Do you want a robe or some sweats or something?"

And now Kat hesitated. Much as she would have loved to ditch that dress, she owed J. P. Harrington enough already, too much really, without raiding his closet. "Thanks, but I think I'll stick with what I've got."

What there was of it, Kat thought, sliding the dress over her head. What had been perfectly appropriate for a night on the town lacked a certain modesty for daylight. Not to mention the wrinkles. Or her wet hair.

What the hell, the man had seen her with her head hanging over a toilet. It was a little late to be worried about appearances at this point.

Head high, she sailed out. "Coffee. I owe you another thanks."

"You're welcome, again."

But even as she took the mug, she felt J.P.'s eyes upon her. "I know. It's wrinkled."

"That wasn't what I was thinking at all."

She wondered what he was thinking, then decided she'd rather not know. Spotting her pumps, she slipped them on. "All dressed. You know what they say, Harrington—you can dress me up but you can't take me out."

And the sooner they got out of the bedroom, J.P. decided, the better. For both of them. He gestured toward the living room.

Curious now, Kat put the mug down and followed. It was a lot like the other rooms, she decided, decorated in the same tasteful, understated style that took more than money to accomplish; it took generations.

A lot like its owner, she thought.

She picked up a vase. "Antique?"

From the sofa, J.P. nodded. "Yes."

"Family heirloom?"

"How did you know?"

"Lucky guess." Gingerly, she replaced it, her eyes circling the room. "Well, Harrington, nice place. Very nice."

J.P. wasn't fooled for a minute. He'd caught the little gleam in her eye. "You must be feeling better. You're starting to give me a hard time."

"And here I thought I was being so polite." Hands

clasped behind her back, Kat crossed to the fireplace, where family photographs covered the mantel. Mother, father, and child, all smiling and set against luxurious backdrops. They looked like a very rich version of the Brady Bunch.

One picture in particular caught her eye. "May I?"

"Of course."

It was of J. P. Harrington when he was about ten years old. The picture made Kat smile. "Did you really used to wear those shirts with the little alligators on them?"

"Yes."

"God, I would have beaten the hell out of you when I was a kid. Nothing personal, of course, it would have been the principle of the thing." She'd been so jealous of those kids, she recalled now. Not just for their money, but for the caring those clothes represented.

"I still wear them," J.P. pointed out.

Over her shoulder, she looked back at him. "Thanks for the offer, Harrington, but you're too big to take now."

Somehow, J.P. doubted that. He remembered Kat Kiley's note and how deeply it had cut.

She looked back at the photos once more. A happy family. Besides money, that was another thing she and J.P. did not have in common.

She supposed that was why J.P. was so nice all the time. He assumed the best in people while she assumed the worst. They had both been molded by their past.

Two entirely different molds. But wishing things could be different didn't make them so.

Kat replaced the photo on the mantel. "Well, I guess I'd better be going."

"Yes." His tone neutral, J.P. rose to his feet. "I guess you'd better."

"I...ah...wanted to thank you for everything. The tanks, and rushing into that ladies' room, and last night." Wincing, Kat broke off. "God, this is getting embarrassing."

J.P. stuffed his hands into his sweatpants pockets. "It was no problem."

"Not even the ladies' room?"

"All right, I'll admit I could have lived without that."

"I'll bet." Kat recalled J.P.'s chagrined expression, the one she now glimpsed, the same one that made her like him so much.

"Come on." With a smile, he gestured toward the door. "I'll give you a ride home."

But Kat shook her head. "Oh, no thanks. You've done enough already. I'll just take the subway."

J.P.'s reaction was automatic, as instinctive as his need to keep saving her. He scanned her body with one long glance. "Dressed like that? Kiley, are you crazy?"

In the stunned silence, it was Kat who laughed first. "Well, Harrington, this is pretty much where we came in."

"Yes, I guess it is, but I really can't let you take the subway."

"Tell you what, we'll compromise. I'll take a cab. I promise."

"Well, at least borrow the coat."

"I'm not sure how I'd get it back to you. Besides, I'll be fine."

J.P. suspected she would. He was far less sure about himself. "Well, here's your award. You wouldn't want to forget that."

"Thanks again."

"You're welcome again."

When Kat started for the door, automatically J.P. moved with her to hold it open. And he thought that he could let her go. Was all prepared to let Kat Kiley walk right back out of his life again, just as abruptly, just as inexplicably, as she'd walked into it.

At the threshold, Kat paused. It was impulse, really, that stopped her, that and some other emotion she didn't care to put a name to. "You're a nice man, Jackson Pierce Harrington." Before she could think about it, before she could stop herself, she leaned close to brush his cheek in a kiss.

Compared to the heat they'd shared, that chaste peck wasn't really a kiss at all. Then again, it wasn't an ending, either.

Kat Kiley might be fast. For once, J. P. Harrington was faster.

Embarrassed now, she would have backed away, except his hands shot out to encircle her waist. Firmly, he held her near. "Wait a minute, Kiley. Wait just one damned minute."

Eyes huge, she stared at him. "What's the matter? I thought I was being polite."

This time, it was J.P. who answered a question with a question. "Did you really think, Kathleen, that you were going to make a statement like that, kiss me like that, dressed the way you're dressed and then waltz right out of here?"

"Well, I..."

For the first time since he'd known her, Kat seemed totally unsure of her moves.

"That's what I thought." J.P. lowered his head toward hers.

At the point of contact, Kat stopped him. "I could be contagious."

"You undoubtedly are." Deliberately, he kissed her. "Too late."

"I hurt you once."

"I know. I'm still reeling from the blow." In punishment, he bit her none too gently on her lip.

A little breathless, Kat still held him off. "I'll probably hurt you again."

There was enough truth in that statement to make J.P. stop and consider. It might have stopped him entirely except for the sight of Kat Kiley in that dress. "I'll have to take my chances."

"Why?" Kat demanded.

"I don't know," he murmured. "I don't know why."

The truth seemed to satisfy her where nothing else had.

"Oh," she muttered, "that's a good reason."

At the foolish reply, J.P. drew back sufficiently to smile down into her unsmiling face. "I have to ask you a question now, Kat, and I have to warn you, it's very, very personal."

Within the circle of his arms, she nodded knowingly. "You want to know if I'm involved with anyone, right?"

"No." He shook his head. "I want to know what you have on under that dress. I have to tell you, it's been driving me crazy all night."

Kat's answering smile bloomed slowly, beautifully, as did the little glint in her eyes. "Are you a good reporter, Harrington?"

"I think so."

"Then why don't you find out?"

If there was a man alive who could have resisted the temptation Kat Kiley presented in that moment, he wasn't in that apartment.

Whatever force had driven him to save Kat Kiley in the first place, whatever force kept him coming back for more, whatever inexplicable force pushed one man toward one woman, it drove him now.

This time when he kissed her, Kat put up no protest, and this time when he kissed her, the heat between them swirled again.

"This is crazy," Kat muttered against his lips.

It was crazy. Far crazier than the first time. This time, J. P. Harrington had no excuse. This time he knew exactly what he was getting into, and yet he couldn't stop, even when the woman in his arms, straining passionately against him, murmured, "I still don't want to get involved, Jackson."

"Of course not." Nipping at her shoulder, he reached for the zipper on her dress, even as she removed his sweatshirt to find the man beneath.

When her hands slid roughly over his chest, his hands trembled at the opening.

"Don't rip it," Kat warned. "This dress cost me three hundred bucks."

"I'll buy you another."

But Kat danced away and slid out of it herself.

And one question of J.P.'s was finally answered.

Beneath that dress Kat wore nothing, nothing except woman.

His breath clogged thickly in his throat. "Help!" he muttered weakly. It was a good thing he hadn't known that last night—gentleman or no, he might have made his move, whether she was conscious or not.

"Am I going to have to seduce you again, Harrington?"

By way of answer, he caught her around the waist and swung her into his arms. Settling her on the sofa, he settled himself over her. "Does that answer that question, Kathleen?"

"Not yet, Harrington."

Her eyes took on a gleam he remembered well. Even when he hadn't wanted to remember, he had. "I warn you, Kiley, I'm taking this as a personal challenge."

"Big talk, no—oh, God, help," she muttered weakly,

when his mouth slid down her body to her breasts and his hands slid lower still.

"You were saying?" J.P. murmured.

"I—" She couldn't seem to breathe.

"Are you okay?"

Hanging on to him weakly, Kat gave a strangled laugh. "No."

Suddenly remembering her sickness of last night, J.P. pulled back to peer into her face, making Kat laugh again. "In the best possible sense of the word, J.P."

He smiled then. "Good."

"Except I think I owe you again, Harrington."

With determination in her green eyes, she reached for him. J.P. surrendered without a fight, even when she abruptly switched position, pulling herself on top. Kissing his face, his eyes, her hands skimming down his body, teasing him, exciting him.

He moaned when she straddled him, her gaze intent, her eyes warrior-bright.

Fearless, J.P. thought again. Kat Kiley was fearless. And incredibly generous. Very generous, for a woman who claimed she didn't want to get involved.

They were joined, as close as two people could be. And this time, unlike the first time, Kat reached out to touch his face. The tender gesture inflamed him, more, much more than any erotic act ever could have.

"I don't want to hurt you, Jackson," she whispered. "Don't let me hurt you."

"I won't get hurt," he promised.

Kat wondered if she should be more worried about

herself. As J.P. thrust into her, his motions as exciting as they were sure, she felt as if he'd touched her heart—something she'd never even thought she had.

BETWEEN THE HEAT of their bodies and the narrowness of the sofa, it was a wonder they hadn't killed each other, J.P. thought later, as he lay on his back with Kat wrapped in his arms. They'd taken living dangerously to new extremes.

Still, remembering the way Kat had run away last time, J.P. deliberately kept it light this time.

"Well, Kiley." He planted a kiss in her wildly tangled hair. "I'll consider myself thanked. Tell me something, did you wear that dress just to drive me crazy?"

"How did you know?" Her hands stroked his bare back, savoring the feeling of skin against skin, the closeness of his body against hers.

"Lucky guess."

At his dry tone, she smiled and lifted herself to look at him. "Tell me something, Harrington. Did you carry me home just to make love to me?"

"I thought it was just sex."

Though he'd meant to keep it light, he couldn't seem to resist the opening.

For long seconds, Kat stared at him. Then, just as deliberately, she looked away. "Do you want to fight, Jackson?"

"No. You'd probably win." Besides which, J.P. didn't think he could muster up much of an effort at the moment. "Let's eat first. Then we can fight."

Disentangling himself from the sofa, J.P. reached for his clothes and located her dress instead. Holding it up, he grinned at the wrinkles. "I don't think you'll be going home in this, Kiley. Here."

He tossed her his sweatpants and T-shirt, then he wandered to the bedroom to retrieve new clothing.

"Sorry," he called over his shoulder. "You're on your own in terms of underwear and shoes."

When he reemerged, attired now in jeans and a sweater, Kat was still standing there.

"Hey." He crossed to her. "I thought you were getting dressed. That is, of course, unless you want to get seduced again."

"I attacked you, Harrington."

"We'll compromise. This time was a dead heat, Kathleen." He pulled the T-shirt over her head himself.

"Kathleen," she mused, her wet hair all the more tousled as she smiled up at him. "Nobody ever calls me that. Nobody but my mother."

"How come she couldn't make it last night?" Tugging on her sweats, he smiled at the baggy fit, then reached for the strings. "Is she sick?"

"Only by association. My father's an alcoholic."

Astonished at what had slipped out, Kat caught her breath. She had never willingly told that to anyone before. And the most amazing thing was, nothing happened. J.P. just calmly finished tying the drawstring.

"Well..." Kat refused to look at him. "You certainly took that in stride."

He tilted his head, trying to see her face. "Did you think I'd be shocked?"

"I don't know." Deliberately, she trained her gaze on some far point. "Why? Are you?"

Now, he gently lifted her chin to look into her eyes. "Kat, I knew already." When she glanced at him sharply, he started over. "I don't mean I knew. What I meant was I guessed. Come on, Kat. You don't drink. It had to be something like that."

"Well." She let out a shaky breath. "I can see you had me figured out all along, didn't you?"

"Not likely, Kathleen. The truth is, you've kept me guessing at every minute. And what's more," he chucked her under the chin, "you know it."

She smiled a little at that.

"Do you want to talk about it?" he asked quietly.

She shook her head.

J.P. leaned forward to kiss her gently on the brow. "I'm glad you told me."

Kat only wished she could be as confident. She recognized now that strange feeling she'd had before. J.P. was right. It wasn't the sex that got to her. It was the intimacy, the sharing, the closeness. The trust. She swallowed hard.

It wasn't something she'd ever felt with a man before. And the truth was, she wasn't sure she liked feeling it even now. Or maybe the truth was she liked it too much.

She'd been seduced by the intimacy between them, weakened by it to the point she'd told him something she'd never told another living soul. That in and of itself was terrifying.

"I have to go."

"Kat—"

"No, I have to go. Really. I have a plane to catch at two and I still have to pack."

"What time?"

"Two. Out of Kennedy."

J.P. glanced down at his expensive watch, then frowned. "We may have a small problem. It's twelve o'clock."

"What?" Kat shook her head. "It can't be."

"I'm sorry, it is."

"Oh, great. This is just great." Like the crazy woman J.P. had always accused her of being, Kat stormed around the apartment, gathering up her things. Even as she did, she spared him an accusing glance. "I thought you didn't get in the way of my work, Harrington. I don't suppose I have to point out you're two for two now."

Sighing, J.P. stopped her with a hand on her arm. Calmly, he gathered up the rest of her belongings, then propelled her toward the door. "Come on, Kiley, we'll fight about this on the way to the airport. I'll drive you."

"I have to go to my—"

"Apartment first," he finished, foregoing the elevator for the stairs. "I know. And I suppose you live miles from here."

"Another planet entirely," she assured him, smiling a little in anticipation of his reaction to her neighborhood.

And J. P. Harrington thought he had her pegged. Just wait until the preppie met the urban jungle.

They streaked across the parking garage. "You are not a dull date, Kathleen." He smiled at the noisy clatter she made. "That's a very eclectic look you have there. Sweatpants and high-heeled black pumps. Very avant-garde."

"Maybe you should have stuck with that blonde."

"I told you—"

"See whoever you want, Harrington. You're free to do as you please."

Right, J.P. thought, unlocking the passenger door of his car.

A car that made Kat's eyes gleam. "Nice basic ground transportation, Harrington."

He swung open the door. "You were in it last night."

"And I didn't comment upon the genuine leather seats? The real wood interior?"

"No." He swung the door shut, then entered the driver's side. "You were sick at the time."

"I'm feeling much better now."

"Yes, I can see that." He twisted the key in the ignition. "And laugh all you want, this car can do zero to sixty in no time."

"I hope so." She raised a dubious brow. "Because I now have less than two hours to drive uptown, pack and make it out to the airport. And if I don't—" she smiled sweetly at him "—I'm going to make you very, very sorry."

J.P. believed her. As he floored the accelerator, the

small car rocketed from its space. The abrupt motion threw Kat momentarily back against the seat.

As she righted herself, he smiled. "Satisfied, Kiley?"

"Very."

"Where to, Kathleen?"

She gave an address in a part of the city that made him stop laughing. "Where?"

"I told you, another planet entirely." Her eyes gleamed. "Want me to take a cab?"

"No. Live dangerously, I always say."

Kat laughed. "You've never said anything remotely like that in your entire life, Jackson Pierce Harrington."

"I'm making up for lost time." Literally. Downshifting, he sent the little roadster sailing out onto Park, cutting off a cabbie, who promptly gave him the finger.

He was getting good at this. Confidence building, he shot onto the FDR Drive, and just merged. It was something all the driving books recommended for New York traffic, but which he had never personally worked up the guts to try. Amazingly enough, it worked.

Beside him, Kat blanched as a delivery van swerved out of their lane to avoid them. "Let's not get too cocky, Harrington, all right? This is not exactly a tank. This is a car, a very small car."

And feeling smaller every moment.

Behind the wheel, J.P. just smiled. "Obviously, you've never been a man in a women's bathroom."

Under Kat's direction he pulled off the Drive. Out the window, the scenery immediately changed. J. P. Harrington quickly lost some of his cockiness. "Are you sure this is the right way?"

"Positive."

That was what he was afraid of. "Lock your door."

"It wouldn't help."

No, he thought, it probably wouldn't. War was not confined to Central American jungles, he saw now. There was a war going on right on these mean streets.

It was a part of the city he'd only previously read about. Personally, he could have skipped this part of the tour. "How much farther?"

"Turn here."

J.P. thought anything would have to be an improvement—he was wrong.

A gang of youths strolled down the street as if they owned the place. J.P. thought they just might; they refused to yield even for his car.

"Pull in," Kat directed. "It's the building right there."

Following her gaze, J.P. looked out at the gray, dingy building, then swallowed hard. It was a good thing Kat Kiley was a combat photographer. She could use the skills around this place.

J.P. tried to think of something tactful to say. For all his polite upbringing, nothing the least bit diplomatic sprang to mind.

"Oh, don't worry, Harrington," she replied airily. "I only live here spring, summer, winter and fall. The rest of the seasons I can be found in the Hamptons, Bar Harbor, or the Caribbean when it gets cold."

"In other words, it's none of my business."

"In other words, it's all I can afford." At that little admission, she bit her lip. "Damn it, Harrington, how do you manage to pry all this stuff out of me? You must be a good reporter."

He must be. And as a good reporter, and an intensely curious man, particularly where this woman was concerned, he was dying to get inside that apartment and see her work. "I'll walk you in."

"And check out my photography, I suppose?"

"N—" He shook his head. As always, Kat was two steps ahead of him.

"I'm still not ready, J.P."

That from a woman who had made passionate love to him only a half hour earlier.

Kat seemed to read his expression. "Don't take it personally, all right, Harrington? This is my private work, my art. When an artist lets you see their work, it's like letting you look into their—"

She stopped then, realizing what she was about to say and to whom.

"Soul?"

"Yes."

And here he thought he owned that already. J.P. wanted to ask her then how showing him her work could possibly be more risky, more dangerous, than the way she opened herself up to him when they made love. How could that possibly be more intimate than what they shared when their two bodies joined?

But he didn't ask. He was afraid that Kat would tell

him the truth, at least her version of it. That they didn't make love, they had sex.

At his sigh, Kat touched his face. "J.P."

"Okay. I'll wait here, but I warn you, if you're not out in five minutes I'm calling 911."

"J.P." She slammed the door. "I can take care of myself."

"Who's worried about you? It's me I'm concerned about."

He was only half joking.

"Five minutes," she promised. With a small smile, she dashed off.

Kat was as good as her word. Even before J.P. had time to worry, she was stowing her gear in the back of the little car.

"How much time do we have?"

He glanced at his watch, then winced. "Get in, Kathleen. You don't want to know."

As the roadster rocketed toward Long Island and the airports, Kat smiled over at him. "This is incredibly nice of you, Jackson."

"Incredibly." With a sideways smile, he reached for her hand. Instead of pulling away, Kat tightened her grip on his and left it there.

"We should make it in plenty of time," J.P. commented as they sailed over the bridge.

Famous last words. With that, they hit a bottleneck of weekend drivers out for a leisurely Saturday spin.

"Damn it," J.P. swore. "Move."

But the leisurely were not to be rushed. Beside him, Kat squirmed. "Do something, Harrington."

"What would you suggest?" He frowned at his watch. "Kat, look, I'm sorry, but I don't think we're going to make that flight."

"We have to. Look yourself, Harrington. I'm getting on that plane. Maybe you don't need the money, but my mother does."

He looked over then and caught Kat's expression of chagrin. A woman who lived in an apartment like that, in a neighborhood like that, and she gave her family money?

"Oh, now, don't go thinking I'm a nice person, Jackson, because I'm not."

"Fine, I won't." He shifted the gears. "Just look out for cops, would you?"

"Why?"

He answered by pulling over to the median strip. Freed, the small car roared to life.

Beside him, Kat smiled. "You really are crazy."

"Thank you."

On two wheels, they roared into the airport.

"What a man, Harrington. Ten minutes to spare. Just let me off in front."

Even as the car shuddered to a halt, Kat was out like a flash. "I can't thank you enough," she breathed, already grabbing her gear. She started to dash off.

"Hey, wait a minute." Ignoring the angry blare of a horn from the cab behind, J.P. got out of the car and moved determinedly toward her. "Aren't you forgetting something, Kathleen?"

"No. I have my camera. I checked...twice."

With an exasperated sigh, he grabbed her by her parka and pulled her near. "How about goodbye?"

"Oh...yes, I guess I—"

She wouldn't soon forget this, J.P. decided as his lips crushed hers. With an inarticulate sigh, Kat wound her arms around his neck. It was J.P. who pulled back, mostly because her camera case was now firmly implanted in his rib cage.

Her hair blew wildly in the wind and he tucked a strand of errant red behind her ear. "You're not going to take crazy chances, are you, Kiley?"

She grinned up at him. "I'm going to take good pictures."

"Damn it, Kathleen." Ignoring the jab of the camera, he wrapped his arms around her again. The longing to keep her there was so strong, it was like a physical thing.

For a moment, Kat clung to him. "Don't worry, Harrington," she muttered against his chest. "I'm tough."

He only wished he could be.

But when Kat pulled back, she didn't look very tough. In fact, she looked dazed and confused. Every bit as dazed and confused as he felt.

And that's when it hit him. All at once. He'd been right to be worried. Not about her, but about him.

Because he loved her. He loved Kat Kiley.

The realization hit him like a sucker punch to the gut.

He loved a crazy woman. A woman who had almost gotten him killed twice. A woman who had dumped him at the airport and never looked back. A woman who, by her own admission, was likely to do the same thing again.

Oh, my God. He hadn't planned his life like this. No, not at all. When he'd thought of the future, he'd thought of a house, possibly in Connecticut, dinner parties, the theater, children.

Kat Kiley's idea of the theater had less to do with opening nights than military operations. Her idea of a good time was risking her life for a couple of photographs. And marriage? How could a man even contemplate marrying a woman like her? Kat Kiley would never live long enough to make it to the ceremony.

Oh, my God.

At J.P.'s expression, now it was Kat who frowned. "You look sick, Harrington." No, she thought, he looked shell-shocked. "Maybe I really am contagious."

"I told you, it's too late." J.P. kissed her again, but this time, far more gently, with far more awe.

Noticing the difference, Kat pulled away. "You're getting involved, aren't you?" Her tone was practically an accusation.

"No." Gamely, J.P. shook his head. "No, of course not."

Her eyes narrowed. "I don't believe you."

"You'll miss your flight." Gently, he gave her a little push forward.

"Oh, my God, the plane." She'd almost forgotten all

about it. So much for J. P. Harrington not getting in the way of her work.

"Look, I'll call," she tossed over her shoulder, then stopped dead, as what she'd just said hit her. It was the kind of commitment she'd never made to anyone before, had never wanted to make to anyone before. *Oh, my God.*

With a look of abject terror on her face, she wheeled away.

J.P. smiled after her, a bittersweet smile this time. In her haste, Kat practically took down two innocent bystanders.

He knew exactly how that felt—to be bowled over by Kat Kiley.

For the longest time, he just stood there. The thought that he loved her was scary enough. What was scarier still was that it was all up to Kat now.

8

"HOW'S YOUR GIRLFRIEND?" Patrice inquired as J.P. strolled into the newspaper on Monday morning.

"She's fine." Shaking his head, he raised a brow. "I think I might be in trouble. I think I love her."

Stunned, the editor dropped into a chair. "Well, Harrington, you move fast. Uncharacteristically fast. And just how does she feel about all this?"

Now J.P. hesitated, the truth warring against his own ego.

Into the silence, Patrice sighed. "In other words, she still doesn't want to get involved. You are in trouble, Harrington."

"I said I *think* I love her," J.P. retorted. "I keep hoping I'll come to my senses. Maybe it's just a delayed reaction to that black dress."

"I'm thinking of buying one myself," Patrice muttered beneath her breath. She forced a smile. "Well, friend, I wish you luck. Something tells me you're going to need it. I'll say one thing, though, you two certainly don't have a romance like everyone else."

J.P. had to agree with her there. He wondered where Kat was right now. He wondered if she was taking crazy chances with her life. And most of all, he wondered if she was thinking of him as much as he was thinking of her.

HALF A WORLD AWAY, Kat was thinking of J. P. Harrington. And cursing him.

She crashed down the phone receiver she'd had raised to her ear.

Ten days away. That should have given her time to get over him. But it had only given her ten days to miss him.

She'd never felt like this before, and the emotions confused her, almost as much as being sick confused her. She had always taken good health for granted. That, it seemed, was about to end.

The nasty bug she'd picked up the night of the Press Awards banquet persisted. She would be feeling fine one minute and then suddenly, wham, out of nowhere, a bout of nausea would hit her. And she was so tired all the time. So tired she could barely pick up her camera.

She looked, she decided, glaring at herself in the mirror, like a woman who had just been through a war.

That from a woman who rarely even got the sniffles.

She was not sick, she told herself. No, she was never sick. She couldn't afford to be sick.

It was stress. Had to be. She needed to take better care of herself. Or maybe J.P. was right. Maybe she did need a keeper.

Catching herself, she glared at her reflection. Thousands of miles away from him, why she was thinking of J. P. Harrington now?

This was all his fault, she decided.

Well, she didn't need a keeper, or a watchdog, or a lover, either, for that matter. What she needed was work. That was all she'd ever needed. She grabbed her camera and clattered down the stairs.

Even as she hit the hotel lobby, she heard her name called.

Though the setting was now Eastern Europe and not Central America, Kat would have recognized that voice, that distinctive accent, anywhere.

"Paul Collins." With a grin, she turned.

The Australian smiled broadly. "Well, Kat Kiley, still alive, I see." Those vibrant blue eyes danced over her. "Now there's a miracle."

"I could say the same." Still smiling, Kat shook her head. "You turn up in the damnedest places."

"Isn't there a saying about pots calling kettles black? I was just heading to the bar. Care to join me?"

"Oh, no thanks. I was just going to—"

Grabbing her arm, Paul swept her along. Before Kat quite knew what had hit her, she found herself cozily ensconced at a table. "I really should work," she muttered.

Removing her camera, the Australian placed it on the table and pushed her into a chair. It was beginning to dawn on Kat why he and J. P. Harrington were friends.

Dragging up a chair beside her, Paul merely grinned at her perturbed look. "Now, isn't this better? Now, we can talk." Those imperturbable blue eyes, the ones that never missed a trick, slowly scanned her face. "So, how you been, Kat?"

Confused, scared. "Fine. How 'bout you?"

"Oh, still dodging bullets."

And so, it seemed, was she.

An American reporter dropped by their table. "Hey, Collins. Kat." His eyes turned sly as they landed upon her. "So, how's the boyfriend there, Kiley?"

Around the room, elbows nudged. The story of Kat Kiley's adventures on the night of the banquet, and particularly a certain gentleman's role in it, had spread like wildfire through the small community.

Kat's eyes narrowed dangerously. "I don't happen to have a boyfriend, Muldoon."

"Oh?" Still grinning, he leaned against a chair. "Are you sure J. P. Harrington knows that?"

"Maybe he should let you get more sleep," another suggested. "You're looking a little tired there, Kat."

At any other time, Kat might have taken the teasing better. Then again, maybe not. Feeling the way she was, the ribbing infuriated her, especially when Paul rushed to her defenses.

"All right, mates—" he began.

"I can take care of myself, Collins." She rounded on him furiously. "And as for you, Muldoon, Babson." She eyed the two in question. "Up yours, gentlemen."

As she rose to her feet, there were hoots from behind.

It was a great exit line. It would have been perfect, except for the bout of nausea that suddenly claimed her. *Damn it, not now.*

"Kat!"

Ignoring Paul, Kat raced into the lobby. There was one thing about a green complexion—it cut through all language barriers.

Wordlessly, the clerk pointed to the ladies' room. Brushing past Paul, Kat dashed in, and not a moment too soon.

What the hell was this thing? she wondered, as she leaned weakly against the wall. A parasite, maybe. She'd heard somewhere that you could pick it up by drinking bad water. Considering the countries she been in, it made sense.

Except she always felt fine after a bout of nausea, as if she hadn't been sick in the first place. Good enough to forget all about it, and push it from her mind.

If only other people would let her.

Venturing back out into the lobby, she found Paul Collins waiting.

"You okay?"

"Fine." She might have asked the Australian about her mysterious symptoms, but abruptly changed her mind at the expression of concern in those bright blue eyes. She had never liked pity.

"Are you sure?"

"Yes." Now it was clear why he and J. P. Harrington were such good friends. Both of them felt the need to save her, even when she didn't want or need saving. Kat shouldered her camera bag. "Just a little tired, that's all. If you'll excuse me—"

But when she would have brushed past him, Paul

Collins blocked her path. Stubbornness—that was another trait he shared with his friend.

"Kat, about what happened in there. The mates, they were only kidding."

"I know. I know that." She tossed her hair. "I just don't appreciate being the butt of the press-corps jokes."

Though clearly ill at ease, Paul was a loyal friend, too loyal to stop without having his say. "Kat, J.P. and I go back a long way. And it's probably none of my business, but you don't have to worry, he's a nice man."

"I know." Tired beyond words now, Kat started up the stairs. "That's part of the problem."

THROUGH SHEER GRIT, Kat managed to finish up the assignment. On the plane ride home, the same grit made her contemplate the situation between J.P. and herself.

An impossible situation. Paul was right, J.P. was nice. Too nice to hurt, as she knew she would.

If there was anything Kat had always prided herself on, it was her honesty. She knew that because of where she had come from, what she had seen, there was a part of her that was blocked off, cut off. Forever.

Volumes had been written about adult children of alcoholics, about how they feared intimacy. Kat didn't have to read all the books to know that was true.

But it was more than fear that stopped her, she thought now. It was that she couldn't *feel* intimacy. She couldn't feel the things J.P. wanted her to feel, would never feel them. It wasn't fair to keep stringing him along. Wasn't fair to him.

No, she decided, the best thing to do would be to end things. Now. Before they got out of hand. Before anyone got hurt.

Being a woman of action, her mind made up, she went straight from the airport to J.P.'s apartment. There was no sense in putting things off.

Even as she emerged from the cab, the doorman hurried forward. She blinked at his bright smile, blinked again at his familiar greeting.

"Well, hello, Ms. Kiley. We were hoping you'd be back."

"Excuse me?"

"Oh, I'm Charlie Riddick, ma'am. You probably don't remember me. I was here the night Mr. Harrington carried you in."

The light was beginning to dawn, an unpleasant light.

"Oh," the little man continued, oblivious to her sudden frown. "It was so exciting, so romantic. He carried you right over the threshold, ma'am, like a bride, he did."

"Really?"

"Well, except for the fact that you were under the weather. Are you feeling better now, ma'am?"

"Not really, no."

Artlessly, Charlie beamed at her. "The whole building wants to meet you. Why, we haven't had that much excitement around this place since old Mr. Wilbur jumped from the penthouse floor after losing a fortune in the stock market. 'Course you probably wouldn't remember that?" He peered at her hopefully.

"Sorry, no." Nor did she remember the other night in question, despite her seemingly starring role.

"Just wait until I tell everyone you're back."

Personally, Kat could wait. It was bad enough that she'd become the butt of press-corps humor. Now it seemed the entire borough of Manhattan found her hilarious, probably the entire state of New York.

Any hope of a quiet, rational conversation with J.P. vanished like so much smoke.

"Look, Charlie." She crooked a finger, beckoning him near. "I'd really like to surprise Mr. Harrington tonight. Do you think I could just go up?"

For a moment, the little man hesitated. "Well, it's against all the rules, but—" he beamed "—I'm sure he'll want to see you."

Somehow, Kat doubted it. She doubted it very much.

As the elevator climbed, so did her temper. The press corps, a doorman. It was all too much for Kat. What had happened to Kat Kiley—the woman who'd always been in control of her life and her destiny?

Well, she was back in control now, whether J. P. Harrington liked it or not.

Finding his apartment, Kat rang the buzzer once, then again and again. By the time the door finally yielded, Kat's fury knew no bounds.

Without bothering to look at him, Kat launched her

first missile. "All right, Harrington, be warned. We're about to have a fight. A big one."

"Kat!" J.P. blinked sleepily.

"Oh." It was only then that Kat realized it was two o'clock in the morning. "Oh, I woke you," she muttered foolishly.

"No. No." Valiantly, J.P. forced his eyes open and tried to look oriented. "I was just reading."

At the pitiful attempt, fondness edged out the worst of Kat's anger. She shook her head. "You are a terrible liar, Jackson Pierce Harrington. It must be those prep-school manners of yours."

His answering smile spread slowly. "So, Kiley, did you come all this way just to insult me?"

"Of course." She tossed her hair. "How else would you know it was me?"

It wasn't just sex, J.P. knew then, because he wasn't even touching her. And it couldn't be that black dress, because in its place Kat wore a bulky jacket, ripped jeans and combat boots.

No, he loved her. Really loved her.

The for better or worse kind. The in sickness and in health kind. At that, he frowned slightly. "How do you feel?"

Terrible. "Fine."

"Did you miss me?"

Miserably. "Of course not."

Smiling, J.P. shook his head. "Why didn't you call me?"

"Because you don't own me."

And when he opened his arms, Kat walked straight into them. She couldn't seem to help herself, couldn't seem to stop herself.

Suddenly her plans, her anger, seemed very far away.

His grip tightened around her. "I missed you." He pulled off her jacket to pull her nearer still.

"I can tell." Kat grinned and slid her hands under his sweatshirt. His skin felt warm to the touch, the warmth of sleep, and of security, and of comfort. Deliberately, her fingers skimmed over the bare skin of his back, then wandered forward. Beneath her light touch, his stomach muscles contracted.

Though he didn't stop that hand, J.P. did arch a brow. "I thought we were going to fight."

"Later," Kat breathed. "Let's fight later."

As they sank to the floor, J.P. couldn't seem to find a single argument against that.

WEARING ONLY a satisfied smile, J.P. surveyed the wild confusion of clothing that now dotted his foyer. "Next time, Kiley, let's try to make it to the bed, all right?"

Beside him, Kat yawned. "Why?"

She had a point there. Relieving her of his weight, he shifted to study her. "Not that I'm complaining mind you, but how did you get past the doorman, anyway?"

He watched as a delicate blush stole over Kat's face.

"He remembered me," she muttered.

"Ah, Charlie." J.P. had thought he'd get kicked out of the building for that little adventure. Instead, he found his stock had gone up immeasurably. One old boy had even inquired if Kat had a sister. "I'll bet he did."

At that, she glanced up sharply. "Stop grinning, Harrington, it's not funny. You should hear what the press corps has to say about all this. I practically had to rearrange Muldoon's and Babson's faces for them."

That he could well imagine. "Sorry I missed it."

As J.P. continued to grin at her, Kat's eyes narrowed to slits. "I'm not going to have to rearrange yours, too, Jackson, now am I?" She held up a fist.

"No." Taking her threatening hand within his, he kissed it. "I surrender."

J.P. wanted to tell her then how he felt, but sprawled naked on his foyer floor, he felt this was not the most romantic of circumstances. Even more, he knew his declaration would terrify Kat.

He supposed he couldn't blame her entirely for that. The depth of his feelings nearly terrified him.

Besides, as J.P. knew only too well, guerrilla tactics always worked best with Kathleen Kiley. A man had to keep two moves ahead of her. Rising from the floor, he located his pants. "Well, Kathleen, this was a nice surprise."

"For both of us." Still prone, she gave a shaky laugh. "I came here to tell you I can't see you anymore."

"Excuse me?" J.P. stopped, one pants leg on, one off. What had he just been telling himself about keeping two moves ahead of her?

At his expression, Kat sighed. "And now I've insulted you."

"Kiley, in most social circles, when a woman tells a man she's going to dump him, it's generally considered an insult."

"I guess we don't move in the same social circles, then. And it would be for your own good."

"Oh, and it's so charming the way you're always so concerned about my feelings, even as you're trampling all over them."

He pulled on his pants. This was the kind of conversation a man wanted to be dressed for.

Kat sank back, her head hitting the floor with a little bang. This conversation wasn't going at all the way she'd planned. Big surprise there. "I shouldn't have come here tonight. I'm too tired to fight with you."

His expression grew concerned. "Are you sure you're all right?"

"Yes," she said firmly, daring him to state otherwise.

J.P. shook his head. "When was the last time you ate?"

"I don't know." Dully, she shrugged. "On the plane, I guess." No, on the plane she'd been too busy planning her little breakup speech—the one she'd yet to deliver. "This morning, maybe."

"Kiley." J.P. held out his hand. "Come on, I'll feed you—" a touch of dryness entered his tone "—then you can dump me."

"And you're always so nice about things." She never could get over that.

"Sorry, it's a congenital defect."

"Like your name?" she teased.

"Yes, like my name, Kathleen."

When he reached out to her, Kat put her hand in his. Her mother would love him, she thought. Even when angry, J. P. Harrington couldn't help playing the gentleman.

Her mother. That slowed her movements. "I need to tell you a story, Harrington. A long, sad story."

Calmly, he handed her her jeans. "All right."

With suddenly nervous fingers, she fumbled pulling them on.

Immediately he moved to help her. "Maybe you should eat first?"

Kat nodded. This was not the kind of story a person wanted to tell on an empty stomach. Not the kind of story she cared to tell at all. Except she owed him.

Turning, J.P. started for the kitchen. "Why don't you stretch out on the sofa—" He broke off when Kat trailed him. "Or you can come with me."

The room was as well-appointed as the rest of the apartment. In it, J. P. Harrington moved with his usual quiet competence. "Are eggs okay? I make a pretty good omelette."

Kat didn't doubt it for a minute. "Fine." She watched as he handled a skillet with practiced ease. "I can barely cook myself. I'm not very domesticated, I'm afraid."

When he said nothing she narrowed her eyes. "I take it that doesn't come as a surprise."

"It doesn't." Measuring coffee, he shook his head. "Kiley, you're barely housebroken."

Despite herself, Kat had to laugh. J.P. laughed a little himself, then.

Still chuckling, she slid off the stool. "At least, I can pour out two mugs."

"Sit." He pushed her into a chair. "And eat before it gets cold."

"Thanks. It looks delicious." Though she picked up a fork, Kat found she couldn't take a bite.

"I thought you were hungry."

She looked away from those probing gray eyes, eyes that asked far too many questions. "I think I'm a little nervous."

J.P.'s face turned grim. Putting down his cup, he gestured with his hand. "Fire when ready, Kathleen."

She looked up sharply. "This isn't an attack on you, J.P. This is about me."

He looked at her for long seconds, then nodded slowly. "Do you want to go into the living room?"

"Yes, please."

It was the worst kind of coward who stalled. Kat had always hated cowardly acts. She preferred to face things headfirst and straight on. Yet, as J.P. took a spot on the sofa, Kat found herself wandering toward the mantel, the one with all the family photographs.

She doubted a man with a background like his, a man with a name like Jackson Pierce, would ever understand, could ever understand, a woman with a background like hers. She wondered how to say it graciously.

"Kat?"

There was no easy way to say it, she thought, except just to say it. Fighting nerves, she turned to face him.

"I told you my father was an alcoholic," she began. She waited until he nodded. "What I didn't tell you was that he hated us. Hated all of us."

He seemed to want to protest, but apparently thought better of it and remained silent.

"His rage was bad," Kat admitted, recalling the violence that shook that dreary house through all of her childhood. The smash of china against a wall, the cry of a terrified child awakened in the night by the sneak attacks of a madman. "Very bad. But what made it worse, far worse, was that my mother never fought back. Never. The more abusive he became, the more saintly she was.

"I remember once he broke her arm. We were in the emergency room, and I remember begging her to call the police. And do you know what she said? She said, 'Kathleen Moira, turn the other cheek.' And even at eight I remember thinking, why? So he can hit that one, too?

"Do you have any idea, Harrington, how much it hurts to see someone you love in that much pain and not be able to do anything about it?"

Yes, he thought then. Yes, he thought he did. But it was almost as if Kat had forgotten all about him as she paced the room.

"I never understood why she didn't leave him. No—" Kat caught herself "—no, the problem is, I do understand. She felt guilty, guilty about getting pregnant in the first place, pregnant with me. She must have begged him to marry her. I mean, what else could she do? She was seventeen years old, she was poor and she was Catholic. What choice did she have? What choice did he?

"Well, he married her. Jake Kiley married her, and he got even. My mother used to paint, watercolors, beautiful things. She could have been really good. She never painted again. Not once. Not ever."

"Kat—" J.P. would have gone to her then, but she warded him off.

"No, don't be nice to me now. Please, I don't think I could take it if you were nice to me now." Deliberately, she looked away, then just as deliberately looked back. "Do you see now, Harrington, why we can't get involved?"

No, but he saw other things so clearly then. Kat's cocky defiance, her edginess, her grim determination that nobody would get in the way of her work, the bravery that masked the fear. All the pieces slid neatly into place.

"I understand," he corrected gently, "why you're so afraid."

It was not the same thing at all.

J.P. expected a fight at that. Much as Kat must have wanted to, she couldn't deny the obvious truth of her terror.

Dully, she shook her head. "It's not just that I'm afraid, J.P. It's that I can't feel what you feel. I can't.

There's a part of me that can hurt you and walk away. A part of me that will do it again, and not care."

"Is that why you give your mother money, because you don't care? Is that why you keep warning me off? Is that why you're crying now?"

"I am not crying." That brought her head up. "I never cry."

"Oh, I believe you." He crossed to her then and wiped a tear from her face. "I think it's you who has doubts."

The problem, J.P. wanted to tell her then, was not that she didn't care, it was that Kat cared too much. Had always cared too much. But he knew she would never listen. *Too stubborn*, he thought tenderly.

But there were some things not even Kat Kiley could fight.

Deliberately, he drew her into his arms. Even when she stiffened, he hung on, hung on until the fight fell away from her.

Just as he knew it would.

For long moments, wordlessly, she clung to him. Though she should have felt embarrassment, strangely enough she felt none. Stranger still was the odd sense of peace that stole over her.

With her head buried in his chest, Kat heard the slow, steady pounding of his heart, the quiet rhythm much like the man himself. "You're too nice for me, Jackson. You're too nice for your own good."

But she couldn't seem to pull away.

"Then stay with me tonight," he urged.

At that, Kat pulled back to stare at him, her expression incredulous now. "Have you heard a word I've said, Jackson?"

"I heard every word you said." Gently, J.P. cupped her face. "Maybe you don't need a lover tonight, Kat, but you do need a friend. Everybody needs a friend."

There was a part of Kat that wanted to believe that, part of her that yearned for his strength, but there was a stronger part still that was afraid of relying on anyone, even him. Especially him—because she was afraid she already did. "I can't. Not tonight. I have to be alone tonight."

"Kat—" He tried to keep the hurt out of his expression, out of his voice, but then J. P. Harrington had never been a very good liar, and Kat knew that, just as she had promised, she had hurt him already.

What surprised her was her reaction to it. Suddenly, shockingly, she wanted to fix things, make them better. "Look," she said quickly, before she could change her mind. "Look," she said again, "why don't you come over tomorrow night?"

He blinked. "I thought you didn't let anyone see your work."

"I don't." This time, her green eyes never wavered from his quiet, gray ones. "Not just anybody."

Before J.P. could react, Kat wheeled away. "Well," she said briskly. "I think that's enough melodrama for one night."

Embarrassed now, she grabbed her coat and her gear. Even as she did, a thought occurred to her. How in the world had she come over here to break up with him and ended up inviting him to see her work?

It was a thought that had occurred to J.P. as well. As she struggled with her camera bag, he saw confusion flit over her face.

This time he made no move to help her, nor did he offer to drive her home. "What time tomorrow night?" was all he said as she marched past him to the door.

Kat hesitated. "I'll call."

"Seven o'clock. I'll bring pizza. And don't even think about canceling, Kiley. I know where you live."

By way of answer, Kat slammed the door behind her, a move that made J. P. Harrington smile. Another eventful evening with her. The woman was not a dull date. Now, in his mind's eye, when he imagined Kat Kiley bathed only in moonlight, remembered her smile when she won her first award, he could add the sight of her tears when she'd told him about her family.

And if she thought he was giving up now, then she really was crazy.

9

HE CERTAINLY MUST be in love, J.P. decided the following evening as he pulled into a parking space in front of Kat's apartment building. Only a man in love would be crazy enough to leave his vintage MGB convertible on this street.

Then again, only a woman who was crazy would live in this neighborhood.

Her security system made him frown. There was none. He'd hardly expected a doorman, but an intercom might have helped. And a ten-year-old could have picked that lock.

But when he bounded up the stairs, and Kat opened the door, he forgot all about his car and the neighborhood.

She wore a sweatshirt, ripped jeans and a decidedly stunned frown. "Didn't you get my message?"

He'd gotten three. All cancellations, which he'd blithely ignored. "No, sorry, I was out all day."

"Very convenient."

"Good evening to you, too, Kathleen." Juggling his packages, he stole a kiss, and immediately felt her respond to him.

Smiling, he drew back. "Can I come in?"

"No."

She looked nervous, he thought. And tired, he added with a little frown. "How do you feel?"

"Like a man's about to invade my soul, to tell you the truth."

"It will only hurt for a minute, Kiley." Gently, J.P. nudged her out of his way. He stopped only long enough to hand her the pizza box and his packages. "Here, hold this."

"You really do believe in living dangerously," Kat muttered.

So, it seemed, did she.

Having never shown her private collection of work to anyone before, doing so now took a true act of courage, far more courage than facing down those tanks. It also took faith. And trust. Those last two in particular had never been her strong points.

Not that she could stop J. P. Harrington.

Hands clasped behind her back, Kat watched his eyes roam the room. Unlike his home, it was bare of any family heirlooms. In fact, there was hardly any furniture at all. The absence of things only highlighted the photographs that hung from every wall.

She was ready for this, she told herself. The rational part of her believed that thought. But her emotional side shifted in agony, an agony that increased a million times over when J.P. didn't say anything for the longest time.

He couldn't. He couldn't seem to speak, so awed was he by her work.

These were not news photos at all, but art, works of art. Shot mostly in black and white, their starkness only accentuated the power of the pieces. From every wall, faces stared back at him. The faces of children playing in a park, or by a square in a Central American village. The faces of the old—a homeless man warming himself on a grate, an old lady pushing her worldly possessions in a shopping cart. A soldier weeping and a baby's gap-toothed smile. Expressions of joy and of pain, of fear and of triumph. Kat Kiley had captured the full gamut of human emotions.

And standing there now, J.P. knew Kat was right— her private work was the window into her soul.

Her work also exposed the lie that she didn't care. Only a woman who cared desperately could have taken these shots. Only a person who had known fear and pain, triumph and despair could have understood what her subjects felt, and could have captured it so unflinchingly, so courageously.

Fearless, he thought yet again, Kat was fearless. At least about some things.

When J.P. still didn't say anything, Kat assumed the worst. He hated it. She was no good. Her father had been right all along. She was wasting her time. "Listen, it's okay if you don't like them. I mean, art is a very individual thing."

And still he stared until Kat couldn't take the silence anymore. "Damn it, J.P. Could you say something? Anything?"

Unfocused, his eyes slid back to hers. "What?" He

seemed to finally notice her balled fists and her defiant expression, because at last he spoke. "God, Kiley, you're fantastic."

Still not daring to believe, she challenged him. "You're just saying that, aren't you? I know how polite you can be."

"Kiley, I'm not being polite. You're good. You're great. I mean, I'm no art critic but these shots they…" As though at a loss for words, he paused. "They take my breath away."

She hadn't realizing she'd been holding her own until it escaped in one long gasp. Brows furrowed, she studied him. "You really mean that, don't you?"

She didn't take compliments well, he thought, this complicated woman he loved. "Yes, Kathleen. I really do. Do you want to fight about this, too?"

"No, I suppose not." A reluctant smile curved her lips. "It's kind of hard to pick a fight with a man who likes your work."

"I would have thought so, too…before tonight. It must be that difficult, artistic temperament of yours." Unconsciously, the power of her photography drew his eye again. "You really are an artist, you know."

It was the greatest compliment he could have paid her.

"Thank you," she answered simply. "Is that better?"

"Much." Except for one thing. He turned to face her. "Why haven't you ever had a show?"

"Because I'm not ready."

"Have you ever tried? Contacted a gallery owner?"

"No."

"Kiley—"

"These art shots are just a hobby."

As if he couldn't see the hope shining in those incredible green eyes. "Kathleen—"

"Do you want to fight now, Harrington? We could make up for the fight we didn't have before."

He might have—if he had thought it would do any good. But an argument would not get through that thick head of hers. No, guerrilla tactics always worked best with her. He would backtrack, but only for the moment, he promised himself. "Yes, but not before my pizza. I hope you like cajun shrimp?"

At the very thought, Kat's stomach churned.

They set up space in the living room. The only room, really, besides the kitchen and the bath.

Opening the cardboard box, J.P. doled out pieces on paper plates, then produced tonic water from a bag.

Easy with him again, Kat couldn't help but smile. "Quite a dinner party, Harrington. Not your usual style, though, I'd imagine."

Not from a man whose watch was worth a year's rent. She could so easily picture him in the Tavern on the Green, at Lutece, certainly not in a dingy apartment with a woman in torn jeans who used plastic cutlery.

"Oh, I don't know." He settled easily next to her on the floor. "This has its rewards."

"Like what?"

"No dishes, for one."

"True enough." Cocking her head, she smiled. "I'll bet that blonde knows how to host a dinner party."

"Keep it up, Kiley, and I'm going to think you're jealous."

That closed her mouth. "Besides," J.P. said, picking up his tonic water, "she doesn't take pictures the way you do. To Kat Kiley, the artist." He clicked his plastic bottle against her own, making Kat smile a little again.

He leaned more comfortably against the sofa. "Sorry you showed me your work?"

"Yes." On a sigh, Kat relented. "No. Actually." She shrugged. "It wasn't that bad."

"See? Makes you wonder what a gallery opening would be like, doesn't it?" He glanced over. "You're not eating."

"J.P.—"

"Think of it, Kiley. Your photographs mounted, people oohing and aahing, art critics tossing around superlatives, like visceral and enervating."

"I don't know what visceral and enervating mean."

"Neither do they." He smiled pleasantly.

Kat wasn't fooled for an instant by his choirboy expression. "Harrington—"

All innocence, he looked up. "What? Isn't that what you want?"

"Of course it is." So bad it was like a physical pain within her.

J.P. put down his slice. "Did you take those photos just to hide them away?" he demanded.

"No, but—"

"Of course not." He steamrolled right over her. "So, let's just pack up a few, put them in a portfolio and show them to a gallery owner. I'll even come with you."

He made it sound so easy.

"What do you have to lose?" he challenged.

"Oh, nothing much, Harrington. Just my heart, my soul, my senses. Everything I've ever worked for, lived for, dreamed about. No, you're right, not much."

"So, what's your answer, Kat? Do nothing? And where does that get you?"

His logic was irrefutable. As usual, it got her back up. Stubbornly, she shook her head. "I'm not ready. I'll know when I'm ready."

"What you are," he corrected, "is afraid."

"You do want to fight, don't you?"

"Maybe." His eyes locked with hers. "It would be for your own good."

And now he was tossing her own lines back at her. "Maybe I am afraid, Harrington. But I think I've earned the right to be. Have you ever doubted yourself, J.P.? Have you ever had to?"

"No," he admitted. "No, not like that."

"Of course not. Because all your life people have told you you're good enough. That you could do whatever you set your mind to. Well, all my life, people have told me I'm *not* good enough. Always, for as long as I can remember."

His expression softened but J.P. kept going. "Then prove them wrong, Kiley. Show your work. Show your soul and tell them all to go to hell if they don't like it."

The idea tempted her. And terrified her. "You don't understand, J.P."

"I think I do."

"No, you don't. Without my private work, I'm nothing. If I didn't have that—" Appalled, she broke off then and rose to her feet. At least she tried to, except a small wave of dizziness brought her back down.

She only prayed J. P. Harrington didn't notice.

Fat chance, that. Immediately, those gray eyes narrowed. "I thought you said you were feeling better."

"I am." His gaze bored into hers. "I am. I tripped, okay?"

He glanced down at the bare floor, then relentlessly back to her face.

"I'm a little tired, that's all. Jet lag."

"Is that why you haven't eaten a thing?"

"I ate."

This time, they both glanced down at her untouched plate.

"Are you still sick, Kiley? Tell me the truth."

"What I am, Harrington, is fine. Maybe I'm getting old."

Her attempt to make him smile failed miserably. "Maybe you should see a doctor."

"What for? I don't like doctors. And I'm not sick."

It was a bug, she told herself, a virus. Maybe a parasite from drinking bad water. She was fine.

J.P. stared hard into her eyes. So hard that Kat squirmed. Still rattled by his pushing her into a showing, her temper flew. "There you go again, Sir Harrington, butting your nose into my life. I've managed to survive twenty-seven years without a father, Jackson. It's a little late to be starting now."

Kat watched as the hurt crept into J.P.'s expression. Damn it. She bit her lip. "I'm sorry." She dropped to her knees beside him. "I'm sorry."

But when she went to touch him, for the first time, he warded her off.

The rejection cut like a knife, all the more hurtful because it was deserved. Ignoring his stiffness, she grabbed him and hung on.

For a moment, he resisted.

When had he become so important to her? she wondered. "If I'm feeling bad," she whispered, "I'll go to a doctor."

That made him look at her. "Promise?"

"Yes. But only if I'm feeling bad."

He shook his head. "You do need a keeper, Kiley," he muttered.

"And here I thought I already had one."

Kat had wanted to make him smile, and this time she succeeded. Except the smile didn't quite reach his eyes.

At the disappointment she read there, Kat leaned in and hugged him. And this time, J.P. gave in, his arms coming around her.

"Are you still mad at me?" she said into his neck.

"Yes. Not that it ever does any good."

As his lips brushed her brow, Kat wiggled into his lap. She couldn't quite suppress her sigh of contentment at the rightness of the fit. "You must be crazy, to put up with me."

"I must be," he agreed.

"Tell you what." Eyes darkening, Kat linked her arms around his neck. "I'll make it up to you."

For all his willpower, for all his principles, J.P. couldn't help but respond to her kiss. Any more, he supposed with sudden weariness, than Kat could help putting up barriers between them.

Physically, she was all he could ever hope for. But physically was no longer enough. At least not for him. For Kat, that was all it was.

J.P. knew that there was a part of her, a big part, that still desperately clung to the notion that it was only sex between them. Anything else would terrify her. Though his ego didn't want to admit that, his logic could no longer deny it.

She might make passionate love to him, but he had no rights in her life. None. Not about her work, not even if she went to a stupid doctor. As Kat reminded him over and over, as she proved to him over and over, it was her life. Keep out. No trespassing.

And just as Kat had predicted, that was starting to hurt.

What hurt even more was that her attitude was partly his own fault. Of course she believed it was only sex between them. Didn't he give in every time? She was too tempting, too beautiful.

The heat had always come easily between them, he thought then. Maybe too easily, he added now.

When Kat's hand skimmed under his sweater, with every ounce of willpower he possessed, he stilled her fingers. "I have to go," he whispered.

"Why?"

Her lips trailed a blaze of kisses down his jaw. She was not making this easy on him. No surprise there. "Because I have to be up early." Determined, he put her from him.

Kat drew back to stare. "You're not going to spend the night?"

"I wish I could, but..." He rose to his feet.

"Well..." Kat tossed her hair. "I won't beg you."

Honestly, sometimes Kat Kiley was as transparent as glass. What was he supposed to do? he thought with a shake of his head. Get out, he decided, before she could change his mind. He had no doubt that she could. Had no doubt that she knew she could.

When he grabbed his coat, Kat muttered something about willpower. It didn't sound like a compliment.

Smiling faintly, J.P. circled back to examine her photographs once more. "You know, it's hard to choose, but I think this one is my favorite."

He tapped at the one of the children playing in a Central American piazza, the one, Kat thought, she'd taken the night they'd met. "You are a hopeless romantic, J. P. Harrington."

He cocked a brow. "One of us needs to be."

At his dry tone, Kat had to smile a little. "That shot is one of my favorites, too," she admitted.

He turned to face her then. "At your show, don't sell this one, all right?"

Jaw dropping, her eyes flashed from the photo to J. P. Harrington's face, his confidently smiling face. "I'm not having a—" Though a debate might have been satisfying, it would not wipe that little smile from his lips. Abruptly, she changed tactics. "All right, I won't." Removing the picture from the wall, Kat shoved it into his stunned hands. "Because now it's yours."

"Kat—" Surprised, touched, he shook his head. "You can't give me your work."

"I just did." Staring him down, she crossed her arms. "And don't read too much into that gesture, Harrington," she warned, "or else I'll take it back."

Not doubting that she would, he held it out of reach. She still had the capacity to surprise him, J.P. thought. And herself. Perhaps herself most of all.

You do care, Kiley. Now if only I could get you to admit it.

Slowly, Kat walked him to the door. "I am sorry about what I said before, J.P. I didn't mean it."

"I know."

Her eyes rose at that, then fell again. "It's just—" she shrugged helplessly "—sometimes you make me so mad."

"You make me mad, too. That's how I know it isn't just sex." Before she could say another word, he kissed her.

That, he thought, was a mistake.

"Sure I can't get you to change your mind, Jackson?"

"Not until I get you to change yours." At the beginning of fire in those eyes, he reached out to affectionately tweak her nose. "And don't worry, Kathleen. I'm not giving up."

Then he left her staring after him.

Alone, Kat leaned against the door. First, she'd told a man about her family, and then she had given him one of her private photographs, and then she had practically begged him to spend the night.

Maybe J.P. was right, maybe she really was crazy.

10

"WELL, WELL," Patrice observed. "You're looking chipper these says."

"I'm feeling pretty perky," J.P. admitted. After the past two weeks with Kat, he felt like he could dance on the moon and turn water into wine.

Just yesterday she had convinced him to go to the beach. It had been a blustery March day, the temperature hovering in the twenties. Not a day to be wandering a shoreline. Though he'd been doubtful, they'd gone.

Kat had been right. The beach was deserted in winter and starkly beautiful. Almost as beautiful as she was, with her wildly blowing hair and cold-reddened cheeks. They'd snuggled under a blanket. That had quickly led to far more imaginative ways of warming up.

At first, J.P. had been worried about getting caught. At Kat's urging, however, he'd fallen into the spirit of things.

Now, at the memory, J.P. smiled. He hadn't made out with a girl in the sand dunes since he was a kid. Kat Kiley made him crazy. He had to say it—crazy felt good.

"Harrington, get your butt in here!"

As Ed Lebar's bark bounced off the walls, Patrice laughed. "Well, that should bring down your spirits, J.P. Our beloved managing editor is in one of his I-need-a-Maalox moods."

As always. J.P. rapped softly on the door to the inner sanctum. "You wanted to see me, Ed?"

"Would I have shouted at you if I didn't?" With a sigh, Ed Lebar caught the younger's man eye. "Sorry, I'm in a bad mood."

Moving six months of accumulated paper aside, J.P. settled into the unoffered chair. "Anything I can do?"

"Yeah, as a matter of fact, there is." Ed pushed his bifocals up on his nose. "I'm retiring, J.P."

Even though he'd been forewarned, the news still came as a shock. J.P. shook his head. "I can't imagine this place without you."

"Me, neither." Grumpily, Ed settled his hands over his paunch. "It's my wife's idea. She thinks I should slow down, enjoy life a little." He scowled blackly at the very thought.

In the face of his dark look, J.P. stifled a laugh. "Well, you're off to a good start."

"Right." The managing editor rolled his eyes. "Anyway, I'll cut right to the chase. I'd like you to take over when I'm gone."

"Nobody could ever take your place, Ed," J.P. said softly and meant every word.

"Cut it out, Harrington, before I start blubbering. And here I always thought I'd go with my boots on."

He swiveled around in his chair. "So? You interested in the job? The hours are terrible and the stress is worse. Within a year, you'll need your own bottle of Maalox."

"How can I pass up an offer like that?"

"I know." Ed sighed. "I love this business, too. We must be crazy."

"Actually," J.P. said slowly, "the timing is perfect. I'm thinking of settling down myself."

If one was going to be crazy, might as well go all the way.

He wanted to marry Kat, have a future with her, have children with her. Even if that future didn't include opening nights and a house in Connecticut.

"Well..." Across the desk, Ed beamed. "This is fast."

It was fast. Very fast. He and Kat had only known each other for a few weeks. Still, J.P. knew it was the right move. For both of them.

Now all he had to do was convince her. At the thought, some of J.P.'s confidence faded.

Running a newspaper was one thing, convincing a reluctant redhead quite another.

For a woman who still denied she was even involved, the thought of marriage would be terrifying. Then again, even if he waited ten years, Kat would undoubtedly fight him—to the death, he added, squirming a little at the thought of the battle to come.

Kat would see marriage as a trap. Given her background, he couldn't blame her for that. He wanted to prove to her that her future didn't have to be like her past. That they belonged together, and always would.

"So, who's the lucky woman?" Ed asked. "The redhead from the press-awards banquet, right?"

"Right...only," J.P. set his lips in a grim line of determination, "I'm not sure she knows she's lucky, yet."

THE INSTANT HE LEFT the office, Patrice pounced. "So did Ed scream and rant and rave?"

"Worse. He offered me a job as managing editor." J.P. drew in a breath. "He's retiring."

"Well, what do you know?" She shook her head. "The funny thing is, I'll really miss that rotten temper of his."

"Now you'll have to put up with mine."

"You don't have a temper."

"I might develop one." Grinning, he tilted his head. "I'm going to ask Kat to marry me."

"Oh. Oh, J.P." Patrice seemed to search for words. "Well, that's wonderful."

"We'll see. I still have to convince her." Thinking it over, he frowned slightly. "How do you think I should pop the question?"

"With a big stick?"

"That is not helpful, Mansell."

Everything between him and Kat had always been fast, J.P. thought then. Fast and somehow backwards.

They had made love before they'd been in love, had made love even before they'd known each other. But this time, J.P. wanted everything to be perfect.

And suddenly he knew just how to do it. With Kat Kiley, actions, pictures, spoke far louder than words.

LIKE A GENERAL preparing for battle, J.P. spent the day planning his campaign. First, he set the stage. Then he dragged a reluctant Patrice along to shop for rings.

"What do you think of this one?"

"How would I know?" Patrice rolled her eyes at the long-suffering clerk at Tiffany's. "I don't even know the lady."

"Well, would *you* like it?"

"Yes. It's perfect."

"Then it's not right." J.P. ignored the others' heartfelt sighs. He was only getting married once. Having waited this long, he planned to do it with care. Suddenly, he spied a ring nestled in the counter.

Garnet. A flash of red. Both bold and arresting.

A lot like Kat herself.

"That one. I'll take it."

"Thank goodness." Patrice's relief was short-lived as J.P. forced her into yet another store. "This is not exactly Desert Storm, Harrington," she complained.

"Really? Personally, I don't see the difference."

Finally all the battle preparations were made. Now all J.P. had to do was lure the enemy into the trap.

Picking up the phone, he dialed a familiar number. He smiled at her greeting.

"What?" Kat demanded from the other end.

In his apartment, J.P. fingered a candle. "Were you working?"

Actually, he'd caught her napping. Like a two-year-old, Kat thought, or an old lady—a fact that made her crankier still. "I could be," she retorted, "if people didn't keep interrupting me."

"Sorry. I need to see you tonight."

Kat glanced at her idle camera. "No, I can't. I'm up against this deadline—"

"So am I," he interrupted smoothly. "But we're celebrating."

"Celebrating? Celebrating what?"

"I'll tell you tonight. Seven o'clock. My place."

"No, I—"

"And wear that black dress."

"What? Harring—"

The dial tone buzzed annoyingly in Kat's ear. J. P. Harrington was a man of confidence, she thought, slamming down the phone.

If only she were a woman of energy.

Lately, she woke from an eight hour sleep, longing for a nap. That from a woman who used to survive on caffeine and adrenaline. She wondered if she should see a doctor, then pushed the thought aside.

She didn't need a doctor. What she needed was peace and quiet.

Still, she removed the black dress from the back of her closet, remembering the night she'd last worn it. Her first award, J.P.'s embarrassed blush at finding himself in the ladies' room, him carrying her home, and the events that had followed.

What a night. Then again, most nights with J. P. Harrington had not been ordinary.

She wondered what he had in store for her tonight.

She was almost too tired to find out, she thought as she struggled with the zipper of the black dress.

As she left her apartment, she glanced back at her camera.

He was getting in the way of her work, Kat decided. And he was getting far too confident.

Something had to be done about both.

ANTICIPATING HER ARRIVAL, J.P. opened the door even as Kat stepped off the elevator. "You wore the dress."

And looked gorgeous in it. All except for the matching black scowl that marred Kat's face as she strode forward.

"All right, Harrington, what's so important that you dragged me—"

Her breath caught at the sight of J.P. in his tux.

Did all men look so sexy in formal evening wear, or was the wild flutter of her pulse due only to him? That was one question she preferred to leave unanswered.

With a hand at the small of her back, J.P. guided her through the door.

And her breath caught again. She might not have recognized the place. His apartment was lit only by candles, dozens of them scattered around the room. The wavering flames flickered and danced, casting a rosy glow over the place.

In the grate, a fire crackled cozily, and on the stereo, soft music played.

Kat's artist's eye couldn't help but be captivated by the scene. "Oh. Oh, it's so beautiful."

"So are you." Before she could step back, defend herself, J.P. dragged her hand to his lips. He brushed her fingers with a soft kiss that made her head reel.

Feeling herself weaken, Kat pulled her hand away. "All right, Harrington, what's going on?"

"I told you, we're celebrating."

In the flickering light, she couldn't quite make out his expression, but she sensed his smile. Sensed even more that she didn't quite like or trust that small smile. "Celebrating what?"

"Several things," he informed her smoothly, taking her into his arms. "But first let's dance."

"Dance?"

"Yes, just like that first night. Remember?"

Even if her mind didn't want to, her body did. Unconsciously, she softened against him.

"That's better." J.P. drew her more fully against him until every inch of their bodies touched. Unlike the first time, he ran his fingertips over the exposed skin of her bare back where her dress dipped. At even that light caress, Kat shivered.

"Just relax," he whispered close to her ear.

"Relax about what?"

He only slid his hand deeper into the V of that dress, finding the sensitive skin at her waist.

Kat pulled back to look into J. P. Harrington's gray eyes. They were very innocent gray eyes, far too innocent for her liking. "What are you up to?"

J.P. smiled down into Kat's green eyes. Suspicious,

and somewhat confused green eyes, he thought. "You are a hard woman to seduce, Kathleen Kiley."

"Oh, is that what this is all about? Well, why didn't you say so, Harrington?"

"Not seduction exactly," he amended. "More like..."

He kissed her then. Kissed her in a way that he'd done only once before. That first night.

What Kat had thought was an ending, but had turned out to be only the beginning.

Slowly, lingeringly, he let his body say what he couldn't yet speak aloud.

And even as Kat responded, couldn't help but respond, a flicker of fear built. As she was reminded once again, J. P. Harrington, for all his gentlemanly ways, didn't always fight fair.

With difficulty, she drew her lips away. "You're—" Her voice not quite steady, she tried again. "You're scaring me, J.P."

Because he knew he was about to terrify her, he tightened his grip. "I know. So hold on."

Gently, deliberately, he lifted her into his arms.

"What are you doing? Where are we going?"

"To the bedroom." He smiled down into her confused eyes. "I thought women liked this romantic stuff."

"Maybe the blonde does, but I don't want—"

He only kissed her again and carried her into the other room.

Again, there were candles everywhere, Kat saw, dazed.

"They remind me of your hair," J.P. said softly. He laid her down gently on the silken spread, so gently that Kat's heart caught. "You have such beautiful hair. Like fire."

Sitting on the edge of the bed, he ran his hands through it. "The first time I saw you, I wanted to do this."

"The first time you saw me," she reminded him. "You wanted to kill me."

"Kiss you or kill you." Gently, he played with a curl. "I never could quite decide which."

"It was a crazy day." And a far crazier night. At the memory, Kat smiled. Now that she knew him better, both seemed out of character for him. "I'll bet it was the first truly crazy thing you've ever done in your life, Jackson Pierce Harrington."

"I'll bet you're right. Here's to many more to come."

Even through the flickering light, Kat caught the expression on J.P.'s face. Something about that look caused panic to well up within her again. She started to pull away. But J.P. held her near. "You're not scared, are you?"

"No... Yes." Deliberately, she stilled his hand. "And I've warned you about playing with fire before, Jackson."

"You've warned me about a lot of things, Kathleen."

"And you never listen." Nor, she thought, was he listening now.

"You are so beautiful." He framed her face within his hands.

She *was* beautiful. Incredibly, impossibly, even more beautiful than that first night. The sharp edges that had marked Kat Kiley then had now eased into softer lines and planes.

And even as he bent his head to kiss her, her body melted against his just like candle wax. This was one thing Kat never could fight.

She had changed, he thought. Kat had changed even if she didn't recognize it yet herself.

His hands caressed her gently yet surely, knowing exactly her sensitive points, until beneath him Kat thought she would go quietly mad. Their clothing was a barrier, and she frantically sought the stays of his tux collar.

He stilled her seeking fingers. "Allow me," he murmured.

With his eyes firmly fixed on hers, he removed his jacket, then undid the collar. With his shirt still on, he removed her pumps, then lay down beside her again.

"What about the rest?" she murmured hotly, drawing him near again.

"All in good time." As he lowered his mouth to hers, his hands caressed her from neck to hip to thigh. Still keeping his mouth tightly against hers, he found the zipper on the side of her dress. This time, easily, surely, he eased it down, baring her to the waist—only to the waist, and there he stopped.

The starched fabric of his cotton shirt rubbed against the sensitive points of her breasts. Each movement brought torture, exquisite torture. She moaned low in her throat.

Wanting skin against skin, Kat sought the tiny buttons of his dress shirt, seeking to free the man beneath, the man she knew lay beneath. Except her fingers trembled, and fumbled.

When had he gotten so strong? Kat wondered. When had she gotten so weak?

In the end, J.P. unbuttoned his shirt himself, skimming off the rest of the layers as well, until bare flesh touched equally bare flesh, and they were one.

Heat swirled again, molten heat, blinding heat, that scorched them both. But before the fire could envelop them, J.P. raised Kat's face to his.

"Look at me," he demanded, still moving within her. "I want you to look at me."

Try as she might, she couldn't seem to do anything else.

"It's not just sex, Kathleen. It's not just sex and it never was."

Kat wanted to deny it, wanted to make a valiant last desperate effort to save herself. But she found she couldn't say a word, pinned by the quiet gray of a man's eyes and the rightness of their joining.

This time the room was not dark, but dancing with the warm glow of candlelight. This time no war waited right outside those doors. And this time, Kat Kiley couldn't stop herself from crying out. "Jackson!" Their eyes were still locked as they both reached a shattering climax.

Now, J.P. thought a few moments later. Kat lay drowsy against him, her body pliant against his own, her defenses down. *Now is the perfect time.*

"Kathleen, I love you and I want to marry you."

Beside her, J.P. prepared himself for the fight. Braced, he waited. He expected angry words, he expected fear.

What he hadn't expected, couldn't have anticipated, was the total silence that followed his declaration.

Confused, he rolled over to peer down at her. And shook his head at the sight.

Curled against his side, Kat Kiley was fast asleep.

J.P. sighed.

On a sudden thought, he blew out the candles, the ones he'd lit with such romantic intent and high hopes. The way his luck was running lately, it was quite possible he'd burn down the entire apartment building.

11

"KAT? Kathleen." J.P. woke her early the following morning.

"Hi, there." Drifting into consciousness, she smiled sleepily as her eyes landed on his face. "Sorry, I must have dozed off last night. Did I miss anything?"

"Oh...no. Nothing much."

She leaned forward to kiss him. J.P. held her off. Not this time. This time she was not going to seduce, con or wheedle her way out of it.

Determined to have his say, he rolled over, pinning her beneath him. "Kat, we need to talk."

"That's right, we're celebrating. You never did tell me what the occasion was."

"I'm trying to." He caught the hand that was caressing his jawline, his very stubborn jawline. "Kat, I—"

Beneath him, she suddenly paled, then pushed frantically against his shoulder. "Move, Harrington. Move!"

"What's the matter? I haven't said anything yet."

"Well, it's going to have to wait."

"Oh, no, Kiley, not this time."

"Yeah, it is." With one mighty shove, she freed herself and scrambled off the bed. "Because I'm going to be sick."

J.P. watched as she hurtled toward the bathroom, a clashing symphony of red hair and green face.

Behind her, a thought grew. A grim thought, as J.P. heard her wrenching gasps.

Far more determined now, he made his way toward the bath. Without knocking, he kicked the door open. "Have you been sick ever since the press-awards dinner?"

"You and your questions, Harrington." Rising to her feet, Kat made her way to the sink and rinsed out her mouth and washed her hands. When she would have brushed past him, he shifted, cutting off her escape.

"I repeat, have you been sick since the press-awards dinner?"

"No. No, of course not. Before," she muttered.

"Before?" Incredulous, J.P. stared at her. Mentally calculating, the horror grew. "That's ten weeks. And, of course, you've been to a doctor?"

"Not exactly."

None too gently, he grabbed her by the shoulders. "Are you trying to tell me, Kiley, that you've been sick for ten weeks now? Without seeing anybody about it?"

"Well, if you want to put it like that..."

"Goddamn it, Kathleen." The temper J. P. Harrington didn't know he had exploded once again. "You really are crazy."

Grabbing her hand, he yanked her from the bathroom.

"It's a bug. A parasite." She dragged against his grip. "You know, from drinking bad water."

"And you could die from that. You crazy little idiot."

"Die?" Kat stopped fighting.

"Yes. If left untreated." Or it could be something worse, J.P. thought. Something far worse. Something he didn't even want to think about. And Kat Kiley thought he didn't know fear. In that moment, he understood every gut-wrenching nuance of it. "You're going to a doctor, Kiley. Now, today, even if I have to drag you every step of the way."

He thought it just might come to that. When he tossed her dress to her, she failed to catch it.

"I can't go in this," was all she said.

"Fine. Then we'll stop by your apartment first, but you're going to a doctor." When she just stood there, J.P. shook his head. "Even if you don't care about yourself, Kathleen. I care about you."

Slowly, she picked her dress up off the floor. "Will you come with me?"

He stared at her averted head, at the cascade of red-gold hair that couldn't quite conceal the fear in those incredible green eyes. "Always." Brushing aside her shaky fingers, he pulled the dress over her head himself. "I'll always come with you. Just try to get rid of me."

NEVER LET IT be said that Kat Kiley let a challenge go unanswered.

The doctor's office was busy. So was she...busy complaining.

"Look, Harrington, this is ridiculous. I don't need a doctor. I'm fine."

"Right." Since she'd said that no less than seven times over the last twenty minutes, J.P. had passed far beyond argument. Ignoring her, he buried his nose deeper into U.S. *News and World Report.*

Beside him, Kat shifted restlessly, then tossed *People* back onto the table. "I'm fine." Before he could stop her, she'd jumped to her feet. "Do you want me to do a hundred jumping jacks? A few push-ups to prove it?"

"No." Though several other people around the waiting room looked interested at the prospect, J.P. noted. "What I want you to do is sit down."

When she didn't, he helped her into a chair with gentle but insistent pressure.

"I'm going to get even for this, Jackson. I swear I will."

"Promises, promises." Reminding himself she wasn't feeling well, he planted a light kiss in her hair. "I'll be right back."

He took two steps, then turned. "And don't even think about getting up."

Halfway out of her chair, Kat plopped back down with a glare.

At the reception desk, a harassed-looking brunette reigned. To get her attention, J.P. cleared his throat. "Excuse me, but how much longer do you think this will take?"

"Sir, it will take as long as it takes." But even her expression turned pitying as she caught sight of Kat's glower. "Nasty temper."

"That? Oh, you should see her when she really gets going."

"I'll see what I can do."

"Well, Kathleen," J.P. said as he returned to her side, "it's now unanimous. The entire world thinks you're crazy."

"I must be, to have wasted a whole morning sitting here. Look, Harrington, I have deadlines. Maybe you can afford to miss yours, but I can't. I'm out of here."

Before she could make good her threat, a voice rang out. "Kathleen. Kathleen Kiley. The doctor will see you now."

Kat turned to see a nurse awaiting her, a very official-looking figure in white bearing a very official-looking chart. "Damn."

Kat looked scared, so scared J.P. started to rise out of his chair. "I'll come with you."

This time, it was Kat who pushed him back down. "Please, Harrington, this is bad enough without an audience."

When she would have walked away, he grabbed her hand. "Hey..."

"I have to go."

"I know." J.P. wanted to tell her then how he felt. Wanted to ask her right then and there to marry him. Except one glance around the crowded waiting room convinced him otherwise. As usual with Kat, this was neither the time nor the place.

Instead, he contented himself with a tight squeeze of her hand. "Give 'em hell, Tiger."

"I plan to." With one last squeeze of her own, she followed the nurse into the examining room.

Fifteen minutes later, sufficiently humiliated in a backless gown and having had enough blood drained out of her to satisfy a family of vampires, it was hard for Kat to tell who was giving who the hard time.

Squirming on the table, she watched as the doctor washed his hands at the sink—an interminable process. "So, what do you think it is?"

His back to her, he shrugged white-coated shoulders. "Hard to be sure, really."

Seven years of medical school for that. She would kill J. P. Harrington and his overprotective instincts.

"The blood test will confirm it, of course. Classic symptoms of pregnancy, though."

"What?" Kat stared. She shivered, as if somebody had walked across her grave.

"Well, the nausea, the vomiting, even the dizziness. Very common in pregnant women, particularly in the first trimester." He turned then, smiling. "But don't worry, Mrs. Kiley. You're in good hands."

"I'm not married," she returned, unsmiling. "Nor do I plan to be. Ever. And I'm not pregnant. I can't be. I'm on the pill."

And had been ever since she'd been old enough to cop her first prescription. There was no way a woman with a history like hers would ever take a chance like that.

Approaching her, the doctor donned gloves. "Let's just do the internal exam, all right, Ms. Kiley? Then we'll know more."

As if she had any choice. As she lay prone on the table, he poked and prodded endlessly. It was a vivid reminder of how much Kat hated authority figures. Almost, but not quite, as much as she hated to be out of control.

Squinting at the doctor's Coke-bottle glasses, she caught his sudden frown. "It's a virus, right. A bug? One of those parasites you pick up in foreign countries? It was stupid of me to drink bad water. I need to take better care of myself."

She was babbling. Even realizing it, she couldn't seem to stop herself.

Then again, never had she wished so fervently to be sick.

"Not exactly." Stepping back, the doctor slowly stripped off his gloves.

"How 'not exactly'?"

"You're pregnant. About ten weeks along, I'd guess."

"I told you. I can't be. I'm on the pill."

"No birth control method is one-hundred-percent effective. Look, Ms. Kiley, I take it this pregnancy wasn't exactly planned, but there's nothing I can do except recommend a good obstetrician. Oh, and I'll write you out a prescription for prenatal vitamins."

Kat merely stared. When he saw the expression on

her face, it was the doctor who looked away. "You can get dressed now. Call the office for the results of your blood test."

When offered the lifeline, Kat grabbed at it. "Then you could be wrong?"

He turned then and shook his head. "I'm sorry, Ms. Kiley. I really am."

So was she. Numb, she watched as the door closed behind him, leaving her alone. It was only when she began to shiver that she stood up and automatically slipped into her clothes.

Ten weeks, he'd said. That first crazy night. She remembered then her feeling of panic.

And in that moment, she remembered her mother as well. Was it the luck of the Irish—or just history repeating itself?

Somehow, she stumbled out into the main office. J.P. rushed to her side the instant she appeared.

It was funny, really. Kat had forgotten all about him.

"What is it? God, Kat, you're so pale. What's wrong?"

Of course, he would marry her, she thought then. J. P. Harrington was a gentleman. Hadn't he been saving her from the very first moment they'd laid eyes on each other?

Of course, he would rush in to save her now. He wouldn't even think twice about it.

But how long would it be before he hated her for trapping him? And how long before she hated him?

No, she thought. *No, not this time.*

Deliberately, she squared her shoulders. Automatically, she tossed her hair. "I'm fine, Harrington. Just fine."

He scanned her face. "Are you sure?"

"Of course. Much as I hate to admit it, you were right all along. As always. It's a parasite I picked up somewhere. Bad water. A couple of these pills and I'll be just fine." Airily, she stuffed the prescription into her bag.

If J. P. Harrington wasn't a very good liar, then apparently she was. He bought her act completely. Of course, it would never occur to a man like Jackson Pierce Harrington that a person would lie—with that upright and proper upbringing of his.

Relief washed over him. "I have to tell you, Kiley. For a minute there, I was really scared."

"I keep telling you, Harrington, I'm tough."

But not that tough. Even as J.P. moved to hug her, Kat dodged. She didn't think she could stand it if he touched her now. "Mind if we get out of here? I've never been very fond of doctors' offices."

And she was even less fond of them now.

Out on the street, Kat tried to brush him off. "Look, Harrington, why don't you go to work? I have a lot to do."

"Nope." Determined, he steered her toward his car. "Don't argue."

Because she knew it was futile to do otherwise, Kat sank into the passenger seat of the little roadster and closed her eyes.

She felt rather than saw him climb behind the wheel, felt rather than saw him lean toward her.

No, she thought, with a sudden jolt of panic. As she leaned away, his hand merely grazed her face.

Still, even at the fleeting contact, J.P. started. "Kat, you're like ice."

He turned the heater on full blast. "A parasite. You really need to take better care of yourself."

"Thanks, Da—" At the realization of what she was about to say struck home, she jammed her head back against the seat.

No, don't think. Don't think about the fact that you have no health insurance, that you have no idea what you're going to do next, that you're a pregnant combat photographer. Just don't think.

It was safer, far safer, not to think. On the long ride uptown, Kat fell silent.

J.P. knew those bugs could be killers. Real killers. He knew a foreign correspondent who had almost died, and shuddered at the thought.

Well, at least, they had diagnosed hers quickly. A thought struck him then. Some people, he decided, smiling over at her fondly, would do anything to get out of a marriage proposal.

The instant the car stopped, Kat hopped out. "Don't bother to—"

But J.P. was already locking the driver's side. "I always walk a lady to her door."

Kat winced at the phrase, and in silence, led the way

up the stairs. "Okay, J.P. here's my door. You can leave now."

"All the way inside, Kat. I'll tuck you in."

"Look, Harrington—"

Removing the key from her hand, he inserted it into the lock himself, then pushed her gently inside. "Can I get you anything?"

"Just peace and quiet." Tossing aside her coat, she flopped onto the sofa. "There, you've done your good deed for the day, Sir Galahad. Feel better now?"

"No." He settled by her side. "I'll feel better when you do. Pretty miserable, huh?"

"Oh, you'll never know the half of it."

He took her hand. "Look, Kat, I'm supposed to go away tomorrow. A trip. But look, I'll cancel. Someone else can—"

"No!"

At her vehement response, he raised a brow.

"No," she said more casually. "No, I think you should go. I'm fine alone. In fact, I'd rather be alone."

He knew her too well even to be insulted anymore. "Not too much, I hope." He touched her check. "I'll miss you."

Closing her eyes, she moved her head slightly, enough to make his hand fall away. "I'd really like to sleep now."

"Okay." Planting a gentle kiss on her check, he pulled up an afghan, tucking it under her chin. "If you need anything, and I mean anything, call me at the office, all right?"

Kat kept her head turned to the sofa.

"Kat?" He'd call later, he decided. Just to check up on her, even though it would make her mad.

As he rose, J.P. remembered something else. "Hey, Kat," he reached for her bag, "your prescription. I'll just get it filled, before I leave."

"No!"

Before he knew what hit him, she was off the sofa. Before he could react, she had pulled the bag out of his hands. As if he were a convicted purse-snatcher, he thought with a shake of his head. "Why not?"

"Because I'll do it myself. I can do things for myself, you know."

A faint edge had crept into her tone. A tone he hadn't heard in weeks. Stubborn, he thought. Even to the end, even when she was sick. "Kat, you really need to take these pills. This is nothing to fool around with."

And just as always, J. P. Harrington thought he had all the answers. "You know, Harrington, I'd really appreciate it if you'd stop telling me what to do."

"Kat, I'm not." He shook his head. "Look, you're not feeling well—"

"And stop telling me how I feel."

Something began to dawn on him. There was more going on here than filling a simple prescription. "All right, Kathleen, what's wrong?"

"Nothing."

"Yes, there is. You're mad."

"I am not mad. And before you say it, I am not

scared, either. And while we're at it, why don't you stop calling me that?"

"Kathleen? That's your name, isn't it?"

His calm reasonableness only infuriated her. "Not anymore, it isn't. As of today, I'm Kat Kiley again. And if you don't like it, there's the door."

There was no missing the edge in her voice this time. J.P. felt the first hint of anger himself, and deliberately controlled it. "All right, Kat, why don't you save us both a big fight and just tell me why you're so angry?"

"Why don't you stop patronizing me, Harrington? And you can drop the condescension as well."

"What are you talking about?"

"You really don't get it, do you?"

"Get what?"

"I'm talking about your attitude, Harrington, the same one you've had ever since you first met me. Poor little Kat, poor little kid from the wrong side of the tracks."

"I never—"

"Oh, didn't you?" Oh, God, it was fear that was making her say all these terrible things—gut-wrenching fear, terrifying fear—and she knew just what buttons to push.

"You and your fancy cars and your hotshot little blond editor and your snooty apartment. Mr. Big Shot races in to help poor little me. Well, let me tell you something, Jackson, I was doing fine before I met you. In fact, a hell of a lot better than I'm doing right now."

She saw now both anger and hurt in J. P. Harrington's normally calm, gray eyes. Hadn't she warned him of exactly that?

"Kat, I'm trying to remember that you're sick, but I have to warn you, you're making me angry, very angry. In fact—" he spun away "—I'm not going to have this conversation now."

Her voice stopped him. "No, let's end it."

He turned back slowly. "End what? And be very careful what you say here, Kiley. Sick or not, I just might believe you."

"Then let me be perfectly clear. Let's end this charade. Right here, right now."

"You want to break up because I tried to get you to take a pill? Sorry, Kiley, even for you that's crazy."

"Stop playing games, Harrington. You know what I'm talking about."

"Playing games?" He drew in a breath. "Now that's a funny remark coming from you."

"What are you talking about?"

"I'm not the one who's been playing games, you are. You've fought me every step of the way. Nobody gets to see your work. Nobody gets too close. Nobody gets involved."

"And I told you why. And you're condescending to me again."

"No, Kiley, that's where you're wrong. It's not my attitude that's making you so angry, it's your own. It's not that I'm condescending, Kat. It's not that I look down at you. The problem is, you look down on yourself. Nobody thinks 'poor, pitiful Kat Kiley.' Nobody but you."

"That's a lie."

"Is it? You're always so sure everybody's going to hurt you, Kat, that you have to hurt them first. Whatever happened in the past, Kat, happened. You can't change it. But you can change your future. Except you won't. You're too afraid. Well, ask yourself one thing. Who are you so afraid of, Kathleen? Me? Or yourself?"

A long silence ensued. There was nothing like the truth to hurt. The problem wasn't that J.P. was wrong; he was right, about everything.

"I didn't say that to hurt you, Kat."

She knew that. Somehow it only made it worse. Into the silence, she squared her shoulders. "I want you to leave."

"Kat—"

"No, I want you to go. Now."

When J.P. just stood there, looking at her, Kat couldn't stand it anymore. She marched past him and flung open the door.

And still he stared. "If I walk out that door, Kathleen, I'm not coming back."

Oh, God. She wanted to take it back, wanted to take back every last hurtful word, wanted to beg him to forgive her. But pride and fear stopped her, just as they always had.

And this time, when Kat just stared at him, J.P. strode out. "I don't get you, Kiley," was all he said.

For once they were in perfect agreement. In that moment, Kat didn't understand herself. As she watched

J. P. Harrington's long stride carry him away from her, she wanted to do something she'd never allowed herself to do before. She wanted to burst into tears.

12

HE DIDN'T CALL her, and Kat had known he wouldn't.
J. P. Harrington was a man of pride and a man of principles and Kat knew she had injured both deeply.

The irony of it was, she had never needed him more.
It struck her then that she had no close friends. She'd always been too afraid to let anyone get near.

And so she was alone, alone the way she'd always wanted to be.

Alone and terrified, the same way she imagined her mother had been some twenty-seven years before.

"KATHLEEN!" At the sight of her daughter, Francine beamed, wiping chapped hands on her apron. "Did you bring your award? I can't believe it. I just knew if you could get out of here, get out of this place, your luck would change."

And Kat thought her heart would break. "Ma, I need to talk to you."

"Is it a statue or a plaque? You know, I remember when my watercolor won first prize. Ancient history, now, but still it must be in the genes...."

Kat couldn't stand it anymore. "Ma, I'm pregnant."

Francine Kiley didn't swoon. Nor did she cry. In fact,

she didn't even blink. Too accustomed to hard times, Kat thought bitterly. Another dream shattered.

"Oh," was all her mother said. There was no blame in that single syllable. There didn't have to be. Kat already blamed herself. "Ma, I'm sorry. I know I've disappointed you. I've disappointed myself."

Then, surprising herself, Kat burst into tears.

"Kathleen," Francine said gently. Guiding her into a chair, she wrapped her arms about her child. "Kathleen, please don't cry. I'll get you something to eat."

At that, fresh tears poured out.

No, cookies would not solve this problem. Nor could the church. Francine settled before her daughter to smooth away the tears.

"The man, what's his name?"

"Jackson Pierce Harrington." Even crying, Kat managed a shaky laugh. "If you can believe that."

"Have you told this Jackson Pierce Harrington yet?"

"No." Emphatically, Kat shook her head. "No, and I'm not going to."

"Kathleen—"

"Ma, I can't. Don't you see? I don't want to have him that way. You, of all people, should understand that."

"Does he love you, Kathleen?"

"I—" The question stopped her. Kat thought then of J. P. Harrington's expression that last night in his apartment. She thought about the look in those quiet gray eyes in the flickering candlelight, the words he'd uttered and his tone when he'd told her it wasn't just sex. "Yes, yes, I think maybe he does."

"And do you love him?"

"I...don't know. I'm afraid, Ma. I've never wanted to love anyone."

"Wanting and doing are two different things." Francine took her hand. "You know, it's funny, Kathleen. When your father used to shout and rage, you were always the one who stood up to him. Even when you were a tiny bit of a thing. Protecting the other children, even, God help me, protecting me. And that's a shame I'll have to live with for the rest of my life."

"It wasn't your—"

Francine held up her hand. "No, I'll finish. For once, I'll say what needs to be said."

There was enough authority, unexpected authority, in her mother's voice to silence Kat.

"And that's how I always knew, Kathleen, that you were the most afraid."

Her daughter blinked at that.

"Oh, it's true, Kathleen. I always knew it. That's what makes you such a good artist, you see. You feel things so strongly, both the love and the fear."

"Ma—"

"You're not me, Kathleen. You never have been and you never will be. Don't look back anymore. Move ahead. It's time."

"Ma—" Kat blinked back fresh tears.

"Whatever you decide, Kathleen, whatever decision you make, I'm behind you."

For Francine Kiley, that was quite a declaration of independence. One only her daughter could appreciate.

Kat wiped back the tears. "I love you, Ma."

"You're a good girl, Kathleen Moira." Her mother patted her wet cheek. "You always have been and you always will be."

SOMETHING WAS WRONG. Even from thousands of miles away, even in the middle of a war zone, J.P. could sense it, feel it, knew it. He'd replayed that final scene with Kat a thousand times—no, a million times—in his head and yet he could never get the pieces to fit.

It was fear that drove her, he knew. The more afraid she was, the more she lashed out. Always. And whatever she'd learned in that doctor's office had terrified her.

Not a parasite, he thought. But what? He had to find out what, and yet he knew she'd never tell him the truth.

And that's when it hit him.

Always go to the source. The most basic rule of journalism. It was so obvious, he'd almost missed it. And all he needed was a phone and a phone number.

Without asking, J.P. plucked Paul Collins's cell phone from his hand, a move that left the Australian speechless. "Do you mind?"

"Not at all." Calmly, J.P. spoke into the receiver. "Hello, base. Yes, Harrington, here. I need a favor. A big one. I need you to patch me to a doctor's office in New York."

Beside him, his colleagues exchanged wide-eyed

stares. "What the devil is he up to?" the Brit murmured coolly.

Even the imperturbable Paul shook his head. "Blimey, if I know."

J.P. turned at that. "Gentlemen, do you mind? This is a private conversation."

Too stunned to argue, the two men retreated.

"Hello." J.P. had to shout to be heard above the static. "Hello, yes, this is J. P. Harrington here. Yes, I was in several days ago with my wife..." Wishful thinking there, but on a covert mission, it was always best to establish credentials. "Kathleen Kiley."

"Oh, right." The receptionist sounded as harassed as ever. "Red hair. Nasty temper."

"That's her." For once, J.P. blessed Kat's fury. "Listen, we're out of the country and Kat seems to have forgotten her pills."

"That's very careless of her, Mr. Harrington..." The woman's voice bristled with annoyance. "Look, we're very busy here. Come by when—"

"Oh, I know," J.P. soothed. "You have such a difficult job. But Kat is so sick... If you could just pull her chart..."

The hold tone buzzed in his ear. Seconds later, she was back. "Yes, I've got it. What pharmacy would you like me to phone in the prescription?"

Now, came the tricky part. "Well, we're kind of in the middle of nowhere at the moment." That at least was the truth. From somewhere in the distance mortar fired.

"Could just tell me what she's taking? What antibiotic was it?"

"Antibiotic?" The woman laughed. "Hardly. Try prenatal vitamins."

"Excuse me?"

But it wasn't static on the line. "Prenatal vitamins. And she really should be taking them. The first ten weeks are critical."

Oh, my God, J.P. thought as suddenly all the pieces clicked into place. The nausea, the fatigue, the dizziness. And finally Kat's fear.

He thought then of Kat's mother.

"Mr. Harrington? Mr. Harrington, what is this all about? Why would you think—"

J.P. hung up. Stunned, he sat there. Kat was pregnant. Pregnant with his baby. Ten weeks. It must have happened that first night. That first wonderfully, incredibly, unpredictably crazy night.

He must have looked as dazed as he felt. Paul and the Brit approached cautiously. "Are you all right, mate?"

"No...yes. I don't know." For suddenly, amid the shock, the possibilities danced through his mind as well. A baby. Wasn't that what he'd wanted all along? Kat, a family. Even if it was a little backwards. But then, somehow that seemed fitting, too, for a couple who had made love before they'd been in love. Had made love before they'd even known each other very well.

J.P. looked up then. "I need to get back to the States. Now."

"The States?" Paul, the adrenaline junkie, shook his

head. "Sorry, Harrington. There's half a war between here and the airport."

"I know. But I have to get home. Don't you understand? Don't you see? I have to ask Kat to marry me before she tells me."

Paul and company exchanged long searching looks.

"Battle fatigue," the Brit announced firmly. "More commonly known as shell shock. I've seen it take down tougher men then J. P. Harrington."

But the Australian, as always, had his own ideas. He looked squarely at J.P. "Is she worth it, mate?"

It was the same question Paul Collins had asked him the very first time he'd ever laid eyes on Kat Kiley, right before he'd saved her. The same question he'd asked of him after she'd dumped him at an airport. Then he'd had no answers.

But this time, this time, he thought of how Kat had looked bathed only in moonlight. And, he thought of how she'd looked as she won her first award, when she'd told him about her family, when she'd come out of the doctor's office. "Yes." J.P. nodded. "Yes, she's worth it." Determined, he rose to his feet. "Which is why I'm going home."

"The airport." Paul shook his head. "Now, there's a suicide mission if ever I've heard one."

"I know, it's crazy. Listen, you don't have to—"

"What? Me, miss an adventure?" Paul grinned. "Not bloody likely. Come on, mates, we have work to do."

As the train hurtled back to Manhattan, Kat thought over her mother's words. She'd given her a lot to think about.

And yet as she arrived at Grand Central Station, Kat knew what she had to do. At least, one piece of it.

Hurrying to her apartment, she grabbed her portfolio and splurged on a cab. But as the taxi drew up in front of a chic little gallery in SoHo, Kat almost changed her mind.

It looked so sleek, so sophisticated, so intimidating.

No. Kat squared her shoulders. She was tired of being afraid, tired of beating herself up. If she wasn't good enough, then so be it, but she owed it to herself to try.

Head high, she marched in. If the gallery owner was taken aback by being confronted by a redhead in jeans who arrived with no appointment and few credentials, her work soon convinced him that she was not a deranged lunatic, at least not entirely.

Twenty minutes later, it was a grinning Kat who stood on the pavement.

Wouldn't J. P. Harrington be proud? Her grin faded. He would never know, would he? In her fear, she had sent him away, too.

And that's when she started to run. For the first time in her life, she wasn't running away, but running toward someone.

The security guard at J. P. Harrington's newspaper was far less welcoming than the SoHo gallery owner.

"Miss, you can't go up there."

"I have to. This is a matter of life or death."

"Fine, then I'll call him."

Except Kat wasn't entirely sure J.P. would agree to see her. Not after what she'd done.

As the guard picked up the phone, Kat saw her opening and slipped past him. It might have worked, too, if the elevator hadn't taken its own sweet time to arrive.

Suddenly, she found her way blocked by 250 pounds of muscle.

Still, with her eyes blazing, and her shoulders squared, she looked almost equal to the fight.

It was Patrice Mansell who found them, as she returned from lunch. Before the first punch could be thrown, she cleared her throat. "He's not up there."

Kat whirled around. She remembered the blonde vividly, and sensed the blonde remembered her just as vividly.

She was the last person on earth Kat had hoped to see, and it appeared that feeling was mutual as well.

"J.P. is away on assignment," Patrice said, appraising Kat coolly.

"I have to see him."

As always, the editor was flawlessly attired. Designer suit, makeup perfect, every hair in place. Kat was acutely conscious of her torn jeans and ratty sweatshirt.

"Why?" Patrice demanded with the air of a woman who had every right to know. "Why do you want to see him? He was pretty cut up about you."

It was on the tip of Kat's tongue to tell her to mind her own business. She might well have done exactly that, except something stopped her. Behind all that frosty perfection, Kat sensed Patrice's obvious affection for J.P.

Though they might not share anything else, that was one thing they did have in common. Steadfastly, she returned the editor's look. "I was pretty cut up about him, too." Holding the blonde's eyes with her own, she drew in a long breath. "I love him. I love him, only I was too scared to tell him."

It was the first time she'd said the words aloud. It was the first time she'd even allowed herself to think such a thing. She must have looked as bewildered as she felt, for suddenly Patrice chuckled.

"You must." The blonde shook her head. "Even your hands are shaking."

Kat clasped her trembling fingers together. "Then you'll help me?"

"Perhaps I could patch together a phone line."

"I really need to see him in person."

"Ms. Kiley, not even you—"

"It's Kat—"

"Kat, then—you can't go waltzing into a war zone."

"Sure I could. If you helped me." Kat Kiley had always hated to ask for anything. Her pride would never allow it. But then, as she'd learned the hard way, there were some things, and some people, that were more important than pride. "Please."

The blonde weakened. "This is against all the rules."

Kat grinned. "How else would he know it was me?"

Knowing when she was beaten, Patrice threw up her hands. "I suppose you have your passport?"

"Right here." Kat patted her bag.

"All right, then. Only a word of advice—"

"Be careful?"

"No, that would be wasted. When you tell J.P. you love him, try to look a little less terrified, all right?"

Kat managed a weak smile. "I'll work on it."

Patrice Mansell sighed. "Please do."

13

AS MATCHMAKERS, Paul Collins and company were hopeless. As a get-away team, however, J.P. had to admit they were first-rate.

While the Brit stood guard, Paul shanghaied a press truck. With no clearance and even less protection, they catapulted toward the airport.

Paul had been right. There was half a war between here and there.

A round of mortar fire echoed close to them. Very close. Behind the wheel, the Australian grinned. "A grand adventure, eh, mate?"

"Just get me to that airport alive, Collins." But even as he said it, J.P. had to grin himself.

This wild ride would make a good story to tell his grandchildren, J.P. decided. If he lived long enough to tell it.

Kat was pregnant. Even now he shook his head. How could he have missed the most obvious solution of all? This was quite a finale, even for a woman known for her finales.

Somehow they passed through the countryside unharmed and unstopped. Either they were incredibly lucky or incredibly stupid. Possibly a little of both.

They skidded into the airport on two wheels. Even before they came to a stop, J.P. hopped out.

"You are crazy, Collins."

"Thank you. And for this, I expect to be invited to the damned wedding."

"Tell you what, I'll even make you godfather."

"God—" Eyes wide, Paul stared. "Blimey, you don't mean..."

But J.P. was already gone.

THE ADVENTURE was almost over before it began, blocked by a colonel who was far less easily taken in than a New York receptionist.

"This is a matter of national security," J.P. stormed. "Now let me on that chopper."

"Not without papers, sir."

"What do you call this?" J.P. waved his press badge under the soldier's nose.

"Sorry, sir. This is a military operation. Civilians take lower priority. You'll just have to wait."

J.P. took two steps toward the tarmac.

"I'm warning you. Sit down or I'll be forced to throw you into the brig."

Racing into the airport, Paul came to the rescue just in time, with the Brit in tow. Taking matters into his own capable hands, Paul convinced J.P. that he wouldn't do Kat much good from Leavenworth. And though even J.P. had to concede the logic behind that, it didn't mean he had to like it. Fuming, he began to pace.

"Like a bloody expectant father." The Brit shook his head. "What are we supposed to do with him now?"

"Stall. Stall until—" Paul looked up. Across the crowded airport, he saw something that made his eyes widen. "Remember that bet we had, Rogers? What was the final wager...fifty pounds?" Eyes gleaming, he drew the Englishman by the arm. "What do you say we double it?"

THAT WAS HOW Kat found J.P., pacing. Unaware that he was being watched, or by whom, he might have walked to the States by now.

He looked, Kat thought with a sudden pang to her heart, like a man who had seen hell. And she had shown him the way. But maybe, she thought, just maybe they could find heaven together.

Taking a deep breath, she approached. "So, Harrington," she said quietly from behind him. "Are we supposed to be mad at each other or something?"

At the sound of that voice, J.P. whirled around. And blinked. But when he opened his eyes, it was still Kat Kiley who stood there. The same flashing green eyes, the same wild red hair. Even without her grin, he would have recognized her anywhere.

"What?" He shook his head and tried again. "What are you doing here?"

Grin broadening, she tossed her hair. "Oh, I was in the neighborhood and thought I'd stop in."

"In the middle of a war zone. Are you crazy?"

J.P. yelled so loudly that several bystanders stopped

to stare. For once, he didn't notice. But Kat did. More than a little embarrassed, she glanced around.

Then again, a man didn't yell like that unless he loved a woman. It had only taken her two wars and a few weeks of unhappiness to figure that out. Of course, a woman didn't fly halfway across the world into a war zone unless she loved that man just as desperately back.

"Harrington," she shouted above him.

Several more people now stared. Everybody seemed to be listening, everyone except J. P. Harrington.

"Even for you, Kiley, this is nuts."

"I'm sorry," she yelled above him. "I was wrong and I'm sorry."

"Of all the idiotic, half-baked things you've ever done..."

"I'm sorry," she bellowed. "I'm sorry and I love you!"

Now the entire airport stared.

"...this one takes the cake. This is worse than the time you... What?"

"I said I love you." Hands on hips, she cocked her head. "Do you want to fight about this, too?"

"Oh." He shook his head. "No, I guess not. It's kind of hard to fight with a woman who says she loves you."

"I would have thought so, too...until today." Kat waited for that quiet smile of his, that little smile that always got to her, the one that got to her now. "So, are you still mad at me, Harrington?"

He grabbed for her. "Does that answer that question, Kiley?" Holding her within the circle of his arms, he smiled down. "Even if it was a crazy stunt for a woman in your—"

Uh-oh.

But Kat always was quick. Her eyes had already narrowed in suspicion.

Oh, God, don't let him blow this now. Not when he'd come this far. Not when she had.

J.P. pulled the ring from his pocket, the one he'd been carrying around for weeks now. Before she could say a word, he unsnapped the case. "The first time I tried to ask you to marry me, you fell asleep. The second time, you rushed off to the bathroom. They say the third time is the charm. What do you say, Kathleen. Will you marry me?"

The crowd held its breath.

But there wasn't an ounce of hesitation in Kat's voice, nor in her eyes. "Yes. Yes, I'll marry you."

Despite the audience, J.P. grabbed her up in his arms. "No more war, Kat," he whispered close to her ear. "I've decided to become managing editor of the paper."

"That's good, Jackson. Because I've decided to have a show. In fact, it's all set."

He drew back then to stare at her.

At his stunned expression, Kat smiled. "Well, don't look so shocked, Harrington. I owe it all to you. And speaking of which, there's something else I owe to you." Anticipating his astonished reaction, her smile broadened. "I'm pregnant."

"You're kidding. Oh, Kat, that's wonderful. How? When? Where? How do you feel?"

J.P. could have sworn his reaction was perfect, showing every bit as much surprise as pleasure.

But Kat's eyes narrowed again. "You knew. You knew all along. I know you knew. Don't try to deny it, Harrington. You never could lie worth a damn, anyway." She threw up her hands. "But how? How could you possibly have found out?"

He answered the only way he could. "Shut up, Kiley," he informed her pleasantly. "As always you ask too many questions."

His lips descended to her own. The kiss went on and on until Kat clung against him.

Just as J.P. always knew she would.

Take 4 bestselling love stories FREE

Plus get a FREE surprise gift!

Special Limited-time Offer

Mail to Harlequin Reader Service®

3010 Walden Avenue
P.O. Box 1867
Buffalo, N.Y. 14240-1867

YES! Please send me 4 free Harlequin Temptation® novels and my free surprise gift. Then send me 4 brand-new novels every month, which I will receive before they appear in bookstores. Bill me at the low price of $2.90 each plus 25¢ delivery and applicable sales tax, if any.* That's the complete price and a savings of over 10% off the cover prices—quite a bargain! I understand that accepting the books and gift places me under no obligation ever to buy any books. I can always return a shipment and cancel at any time. Even if I never buy another book from Harlequin, the 4 free books and the surprise gift are mine to keep forever.

142 BPA A3UP

Name	(PLEASE PRINT)	
Address	Apt. No.	
City	State	Zip

This offer is limited to one order per household and not valid to present Harlequin Temptation® subscribers. *Terms and prices are subject to change without notice. Sales tax applicable in N.Y.

UTEMP-696 ©1990 Harlequin Enterprises Limited

Look what Santa brought!

CHRISTMAS DELIVERY

Capture the holiday spirit with these three
heartwarming stories of moms, dads,
babies and mistletoe. *Christmas Delivery*
is the perfect stocking stuffer featuring three
of your favorite authors:

A CHRISTMAS MARRIAGE by Dallas Schulze
DEAR SANTA by Margaret St. George
THREE WAIFS AND A DADDY by Margot Dalton

**There's always room for one more—
especially at Christmas!**

Available wherever Harlequin and Silhouette
books are sold.

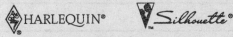

Free Gift Offer

As Seen on TV!

With a Free Gift proof-of-purchase
from any Harlequin® book, you can receive
a beautiful cubic zirconia pendant.

This stunning marquise-shaped stone is a genuine cubic
zirconia—accented by an 18" gold tone necklace.
(Approximate retail value $19.95)

Send for yours today...
compliments of ◆HARLEQUIN®

To receive your free gift, a cubic zirconia pendant, send us one original proof-of-purchase, photocopies not accepted, from the back of any Harlequin Romance®, Harlequin Presents®, Harlequin Temptation®, Harlequin Superromance®, Harlequin Intrigue®, Harlequin American Romance®, or Harlequin Historicals® title available at your favorite retail outlet, together with the Free Gift Certificate, plus a check or money order for $1.65 U.S./$2.15 CAN. (do not send cash) to cover postage and handling, payable to Harlequin Free Gift Offer. We will send you the specified gift. Allow 6 to 8 weeks for delivery. Offer good until December 31, 1997, or while quantities last. Offer valid in the U.S. and Canada only.

Free Gift Certificate

Name: _____

Address: _____

City: _____ State/Province: _____ Zip/Postal Code: _____

Mail this certificate, one proof-of-purchase and a check or money order for postage and handling to: HARLEQUIN FREE GIFT OFFER 1997. In the U.S.: 3010 Walden Avenue, P.O. Box 9071, Buffalo NY 14269-9057. In Canada: P.O. Box 604, Fort Erie, Ontario L2Z 5X3.

FREE GIFT OFFER   084-KEZ

ONE PROOF-OF-PURCHASE

To collect your fabulous FREE GIFT, a cubic zirconia pendant, you must include this
original proof-of-purchase for each gift with the properly completed Free Gift Certificate.

084-KEZR